What the relatives are saying about the newlyweds...

"No, we're not surprised, exactly, that a man like Cordell would be interested in our Jillian. It's just that...well, she's always been a late bloomer."
—Buffy Horton, mother of the bride

"I was sensible in my choice of husband. It's important to consider family backgrounds, bloodlines, that sort of thing. But Cordell...well..."
—Tiffany Horton, sister of the bride

"Well, she'd best get pregnant ASAP. Nothing keeps a man close to home like children...."
—George Horton, father of the bride

"Of course I'm happy that Cordell found someone else so quickly. I just hope he remembered to return all of the lovely gifts that our business associates were so kind to send."
—Alicia, ex-fiancée of the groom

"That Jillian's all right. Those other two— well, they just weren't woman enough for my Cordell."
—Nanna, grandmother of the groom

Dear Reader,

Imagine: you're at home when a carrier pigeon delivers a note to your window. A love letter, perhaps? No—a "Dear John" letter…meant for the gorgeous groom-to-be next door. And *you* have to deliver the bad news.

That's how Jillian Horton ends up saying "I do" to Cord Dougald in bestselling author Cait London's *Every Groom's Guide To…*. The happy newlyweds are just settling into married life when the modern bride learns that her lovable groom is the most old-fashioned man she's ever met. Surely he'll accept a few lessons in "Modern Husband 101," right?

Now imagine this: you're staying in a hotel when you mistakenly receive a seductive little note and a key in an envelope: *"Sweetheart—meet me at the Starlight Lounge at 10—Love, T."* In Kathy Marks's *Seducing Sydney,* plain-Jane Sydney Stone can't resist meeting the mysterious "T," if only to tell him his note was delivered to the wrong woman. And that's how Sydney is seduced on the adventure of a lifetime….

Next month, you'll find two Yours Truly titles by favorite authors Marie Ferrarella and Jo Ann Algermissen—two new novels about unexpectedly meeting, dating…and marrying Mr. Right.

Yours truly,

Melissa Senate
Editor

Please address questions and book requests to:
Silhouette Reader Service
U.S.: 3010 Walden Ave., P.O. Box 1325, Buffalo, NY 14269
Canadian: P.O. Box 609, Fort Erie, Ont. L2A 5X3

CAIT LONDON

Every Groom's Guide To...

EVERY GROOM'S GUIDE TO...

Copyright © 1996 by Lois Kleinsasser

All rights reserved. Except for use in any review, the reproduction or utilization of this work in whole or in part in any form by any electronic, mechanical or other means, now known or hereafter invented, including xerography, photocopying and recording, or in any information storage or retrieval system, is forbidden without the written permission of the publisher, Silhouette Books, 300 East 42nd Street, New York, N.Y. 10017 U.S.A.

All characters in this book have no existence outside the imagination of the author and have no relation whatsoever to anyone bearing the same name or names. They are not even distantly inspired by any individual known or unknown to the author, and all incidents are pure invention.

® and TM are trademarks of the publisher. Trademarks indicated with ® are registered in the United States Patent and Trademark Office, the Canada Trade Mark Office and in other countries.

Published by Silhouette Books
America's Publisher of Contemporary Romance

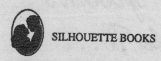

SILHOUETTE BOOKS

ISBN 0-373-52017-4

EVERY GROOM'S GUIDE TO...

Copyright © 1996 by Lois Kleinsasser

Printed in U.S.A.

About the author

Zippy, "today" and fun. That's the premise for my Yours Truly duet, *Every Girl's Guide To...* (10/95 Yours Truly) and *Every Groom's Guide To....* As a today woman and the mother of three daughters (three is my lucky number), I travel and research across the Northwest. I write historical romance under the pseudonym Cait Logan, play with computers, grow herbs and paint landscapes. As Silhouette Desire's Cait London, I love creating contemporary heroes with dark, dangerous edges that only the right woman could tame. Sometimes I wonder if my computer is hosting a cowboy convention. I can just see them in there—tall, dangerous hunks dressed in jeans and boots and Western hats. No shirts. They're discussing difficult, but can't-live-without-'em women.

Perks like readers who care, national bestsellers and awards are pure delight for me. With two separate styles (intense/humorous), two pseudonyms and a go-for-it attitude, I am enjoying myself. After ten years in publishing and a lengthy backlist, I love each book better than the last. I hope you'll enjoy *Every Groom's Guide To....* Have fun.

CAIT LONDON has written fourteen novels for Silhouette, twelve for Desire. Look for her next book, the first of her new miniseries *The Tallchiefs*, in Silhouette Desire in June.

To order Cait's first Yours Truly, *Every Girl's Guide To...*, see the ad in the back pages of this book.

IT'S OUR TENTH ANNIVERSARY!

This book marks the celebration of my tenth year as a published writer. I dedicate Every Groom's Guide To... to my reader friends, who have encouraged me. I appreciate the time taken to write their kind letters. I've felt through the years as a new reader discovered me and read my older books, that we have become a family. We discuss my characters, whether they are in Western historical romances, or in Silhouettes. I love input about possible spin-offs or series that would include minor characters. One reader friend likes epilogues and this book has one especially for her. I hope you enjoy Every Groom's Guide To... because it's for you! Happy anniversary to us!

—Cait

1

——←——

"It's not that easy to resuscitate a dying pigeon," Jillian Horton grumbled. She clutched the shoe box closer to her. She'd had her first experience at bird lifesaving. But Bomber would never see another New York Saturday morning. She pushed Cordell Dougald's apartment doorbell and smoothed the shoe box with trembling fingers. The size-seven impromptu bird casket held the body of the departed Bomber, formerly a carrier pigeon. She had reattached the note with his owner's address to Bomber's spindly leg.

Jillian was the bearer of doubly bad news. Cordell Dougald's beloved Bomber was now deceased. The message attached to Bomber's leg would break Cordell's heart, because he was being deserted at the altar.

She glanced down the sleek hallway of the exclusive apartment building. Outside, New York City was sheathed in brilliant April sunshine.

Atlas, her cat, was the culprit, and had delivered Bomber to her. It was her duty to deliver Cordell's heartbreaking news: he had a dead pigeon-pet, and a bride on the lam. Jillian ached for the doomed groom, and wished she hadn't read the note in the tiny weatherproof case. To fit the paper, the ex-bride-to-be's writing was small and precise. The wedding was set for tomorrow. Alicia was certain that marriage would be a mistake between two good friends. Cordell was to attend the late-afternoon wedding rehearsal and the reception for business associates. He should see that the guests retrieved their gifts. He should pay all the bills and—Alicia had underlined larger block letters—*Be Civilized, Cordell.*

As a survivor in the love game, Jillian ached for Cordell. Perhaps he would dedicate himself to humanity, as she had done.

Corporate profits were bred into the basic survival instincts in her family. When Jillian left her position in marketing and advertising, the Hortons had disdained her charity work and her assembly-line job at the catsup factory. She'd been an outcast, a throwback to her great-grandmother. Grandmother Isobel had given much of Jillian's hefty inheritance to an orphanage. But despite Jillian's black-sheep role, she cared for her family.

She glanced at her watch; she was due at the homeless shelter and food kitchen in the early afternoon. She straightened her Nanna Bear denim vest and the crocheted collar of her blouse. Jillian loved the designer outfit—from Nanna Bear's Honey line of mix-and-match, wash-and-wear clothing. It was the only outfit Jillian thought suitable for delivering the sad news to Cordell Dougald. Cordell would need a touch of softness after losing his bride and mourning his pigeon.

Losing at the romance business was an experience she knew well. She straightened the lace collar and the long, soft denim skirt and rang the bell again.

Freshly showered, Cordell sat on a packing box, a towel wrapped around his hips. The sunlight passed through the windows to touch the small appliance in his fist. Because he was vacating the apartment that he'd rarely used in the five years since his divorce, he'd been repacking the last of his stored boxes from the building's basement; apparently his ex-wife's "personal little friend" had been stored for years.

In Cordell's large, white-knuckled and tanned fist, the conical device whirred, taunting him.

Cordell ran his fingers through his damp hair. Back then, he hadn't thought to wonder about Portia's flustered, warm, drowsy, slightly guilty looks. The device in Cordell's fist damned his manhood. He'd been replaced by sexual technology. He'd inserted fresh batteries in the appliance to prove his suspicions. He'd hoped his theory was wrong. Portia's toy hummed merrily when he clicked it on. He clicked it off and stared at it. Batteries and plastic had replaced lovemaking.

Cordell let his dark mood settle around him. He had old-fashioned values.

He'd come from a poor, struggling ranch family that had never had enough. His mother had aged too soon, her hands rough from doing a man's work. He'd seen his father's tears because he couldn't give a present to his wife on her birthday or at Christmas. Then, at eight, Cordell had been orphaned, bitter that he had been deserted by his parents and baby sister. When the boy became a man, haunted by poor times, he had worked every minute not to return to those times. He had closed painful doors and worked exhausting hours—only to be replaced by a wife's modern technology.

Wrapped in growing anger, Cordell dismissed the doorbell. Portia hadn't seemed to mind their modern marriage. She'd been happy with their prenuptial agreement: she'd live in New York and he'd work and live in Wyoming, visiting for business reasons. Portia had said she had the best of both worlds—marriage to a rugged up-and-coming businessman *and* a cowboy. Her friends had been envious of her life-style, uncluttered by a husband-in-residence. Cordell frowned at the gleaming appliance; until now, he'd thought the arrangement was mutually satisfactory. He hadn't wanted his ranch and life cluttered by a woman's interference.

He scowled at the insistent sound of the doorbell, then launched himself to his imposing six foot three inch height. He kicked aside the packing box with his bare foot and stalked to the door. His fist strangled Portia's little playmate.

Cordell jerked open the door and glared down at the intruder, who was wearing a Nanna Bear's Honey design. He recognized his clothing line at once. The clothing was practical and doing well in the fashion marketplace; a large chain wanted exclusive rights, but he wanted the option to develop his own catalog marketing.

The woman's blond hair was a froth of tiny waves. Her small, round glasses glinted up at him. The Honey design dipped and curved just right around her size-twelve body. He noted that the princess cut of the vest fit her full breasts the way he'd intended. She had the soft, comfortable American look he wanted filling his designs. Portia's and Alicia's rangy, model-thin bodies looked better in business suits.

But he'd chosen both women because they knew about socializing for business; he'd discovered that he lacked the gentler skills. His down-to-basics attitude was a reflection of his hard life. With a socialite decorating his arm and pushing his product, he would be ready for business.

He noted that the woman had opted to leave open the bottom buttons on the front of the denim skirt. This allowed the white eyelet lace slip to show. He'd designed that flirtatious look while picturing it framing legs just like this woman's. The eyelet lace wasn't for skinny legs, but for shapely ones. She'd finished off the outfit with a basic leather shoe. He noted again that the Honey vest dipped and curved in the right places, because his goal in design was to make a woman look feminine and a handful. He found himself staring at lush breasts covered by a Honey ruffled blouse. His gaze skimmed down to her hips and fastened on the soft, round line covered by denim.

She moved restlessly, and he noted her wild blush, saw that her dark green eyes were concerned behind her small lenses. He rarely focused on a woman's breasts—except to decide what cut would suit a certain body type. But a man about to get married—and one who found he couldn't pay a certain important sexual bill—was likely to be out of focus. "What?" he demanded, anxious to lick his wounds alone.

He slid back into contemplating his marriage. Not that they'd had a tender, loving marriage. But it had been a functional and friendly relationship. He glanced down at the appliance in his hand, raising it slightly to glower at it.

The intruder blinked. He noted that she clutched a shoe box tightly against her. "What?" he demanded again.

"I'm so sorry to disturb you," she began unevenly, glancing down his body, then back up to his face. She blinked repeatedly, as though trying to grip her scattered thoughts.

"*You're* sorry," he said mockingly, fighting for control. Finding the sexual device would slaughter the confidence of any aroused groom. His gaze swept down the woman again, and he realized that his five-year abstinence was showing; his urge to make love had leaped to life.

"Ah...Cordell Dougald?" the woman asked in a soft, husky voice.

The sound of her voice locked on to something deep within him. He wondered what she'd sound like after making love.

Cordell stared at the appliance. He felt as though he were on an emotional teeter-totter, trying to comprehend just where he had failed. "Yes. I'm Cordell Dougald."

"I'm terribly sorry."

"Lady, stop saying you're sorry and get on with it," Cordell snapped. He wondered if all women used sexual tools. His experience with the finer points of women was limited. "Do you use one of these?" he demanded harshly.

"I beg your pardon?" she asked, very precisely, after taking a step backward. Her cheeks flushed instantly.

"Oh, hell," he muttered, realizing belatedly that his habit of speaking frankly had shocked her. "What do you want?"

"I...ah... Here." She shoved the shoe box at him. "I wrapped Bomber in a napkin. He looks comfortable...as if he's just sleeping," she whispered worriedly.

"Bomber?" He vaguely remembered Alicia's new hobby of training pigeons to carry notes. She'd faxed him progress reports. Bomber was her best and fastest pigeon.

The woman eyed the appliance, and Cordell scowled down at her. "Give me the box," he said unceremoniously, and took it from her. He went back to sit on his packing box. He pondered his new knowledge about a marriage that had ended five years ago.

"Mr. Dougald?" he heard the woman say. He glanced up to see her hovering at the doorway. "Your bird...ah, the pigeon...was buffeted against my window by a strong wind. I had to open the messenger doodad on his leg to find out who he belonged to...or I never would have read the note."

"Uh-huh. Sure," Cordell muttered without interest as a mocking sunbeam penetrated the window and smote the sexual tool. Cordell contemplated the past. He'd been faithful, and Portia had seemed happy about keeping her independence. He'd hoped that Alicia would fill the position that Portia had vacated—for the president of a vacuum-cleaner company.

Cordell needed a woman to help him with the social aspects of marketing. With Nanna Bear ready to step into a catalog marketing plan, a wife who knew the business-social angle would be an asset. While Portia had not wanted to visit his ranch, she had said she would attend any social functions relating to business. After seeing a picture of his home, she had refused to come, under any circumstances, until he built a new house.

Since Cordell preferred his privacy and his uncluttered, quiet, spacious home—one he'd built himself from native woods and stone—he didn't intend to build a new one.

The woman's soft, low voice interrupted. "Ah..."

"Are you still here?" he demanded, reminded of the box in his hand. He flipped open the lid to see Alicia's

Bomber resting in peace. "He's dead. Cat got him," he said, with the authority of one raised on a ranch.

"Oh, no. I really don't think so," she stated hurriedly. "I don't think a cat had anything to do with it. A strong wind maybe, or smog or kites...balloons...big birds...anything but a cat."

She was probably protecting her cat and lying, he thought darkly. Her expression challenged him. So she was loyal to a cat. And she was persistent. She said, "You might want to read the note attached to Bomber."

Cordell noted her eyes skipping across his bare chest. Women usually noticed him; he was too big to miss. "Do I have any sex appeal at all, lady?" he asked flatly.

When Jillian recovered, she discovered that her lips had dropped open. Cordell wore a towel around his hips and a fierce scowl on a deeply tanned, rugged face. A drop of water trailed down his stubble-covered, rigid jaw and dripped to a chest that spread endlessly before Jillian's widened eyes. Every line of his fit body was taut with anger, and the brackets beside his hard mouth were deep.

He gripped a woman's vibrator in his right fist. The droplets in his shaggy raven hair sparkled like tiny diamonds as he glared at the device. His knuckles were white.

A deep line separated his brows, drawing them close together over fierce, slashing black eyes. She noted the distance between the brows, just as she always did; they were thick, savage, but there was a redeeming space between them. Long ago she had learned not to trust men with one connected eyebrow.

She had seen one or two men with towels slung around their hips, and this man made them look sluggish, pale, and bloated with fat grams. She quivered a bit, and glanced at the gleaming, taut line of his broad shoulders. She blinked up at the man. Marsh had begun to sprout hair on his slumped shoulders just before she discovered his infidelity. Her ex-husband—the perfect choice of her family—had left her with an instant dislike of men with single eyebrows and hairy shoulders. Involuntarily she glanced down to the man's tanned, flat belly; Marsh's tummy had been jiggly, his towel forced to curve under his paunch. She swallowed and flushed. Viewing a near-naked man who looked as if he wanted to throttle her caused her to stutter. "I . . . uh. . . ."

"Do you use one or not?" he repeated. "It's not a hard question." He shot the words at her, rapid-fire. She prayed the towel tucked around his hips wouldn't slip.

He smiled nastily, clearly unwilling to back away from his outrageous demand. "Have you ever used one of these?" Anger vibrated in his low, clipped tone, which was wrapped in a western twang. The low, ominous sound could have been issued by a gunfighter calling for a showdown.

"No," she answered. But her friends had advised her to buy a stress reliever after her divorce.

He glowered at the appliance in his fist, apparently locked in a storm of thoughts.

He shook his head, and water droplets flew through the shaft of sunlight coming through the window. She noted that the muscles on his chest jumped each time he moved.

He turned and presented Jillian with a view of his broad, droplet-covered, well-tanned shoulders. Muscles rippled down his back, all the way to the slipping towel. As he padded through the apartment, she noted the hard, firm shape of his buttocks and his athletic, long, tanned legs. He reminded her of a wounded panther, disturbed in his lair and now padding gracefully back into the shadows.

She couldn't leave him to grieve over Bomber and discover his heartache alone—and he might not open the message carton tied to Bomber's leg. Jillian swallowed the tight wad of emotion clogging her throat. Cordell might show up for his wedding-rehearsal dinner tonight, totally unprepared for Alicia's desertion. She had to help Cordell through his emotional turmoil. Then she would leave him to deal with the ashes of his life. "Ah...Mr. Dougald," she began hesitantly. "I think you might be interested in Bomber's message."

He didn't appear to hear her; she eased inside the apartment. Cordell was wrapped in thought. He sat slowly on a packing box, holding the box on his lap with one hand and studying the appliance with the other.

Jillian couldn't leave him alone; Cordell had yet to discover his worst blow. She stepped over a pair of well-worn western boots on her way to him. She prayed those boots had never been fitted with spurs.

"Ah...I had to read the message clipped to his leg to find his owner," she said. Cordell continued contemplating the appliance. The device whirred in his large hand, and his scowl deepened. Cordell muttered a curse and inhaled slowly. The towel slipped, and Jillian glanced at the dark skin at his hip briefly. She shivered; he was tanned all over. She couldn't picture him in a tanning bed; he wouldn't fit. "Cordell...um, you really should read the message," she urged as the device hummed in his hand.

He clicked it off and shook his head. "I was divorced five years ago, and just found this thing in my storage boxes. It's my ex-wife's. I'm a regular guy. I've been to strip joints. I'm thirty-eight years old. I've never seen one of these," he muttered in a distracted tone.

He flipped open the casket-box. He placed the sexual device on his lap, scowled down at it, then slammed it down on the top of a crate. Jillian's hands found the soft leather of the expensive, very long couch. Her fingers dug into the leather upholstery as he unrolled Alicia's message.

After scanning it, he picked up the device. It whirred for a moment as Cordell stared off into the New York sunshine. He was clearly a stunned man.

Jillian's heart ached for him. He looked so alone and hurting. All her senses told her to hug him; she sensed that Cordell was not a touchy-feely man. She gripped the leather tightly for an anchor. "I'm sorry," she whispered huskily.

"I don't understand. We were compatible in business. She knew I wanted a replacement wife when she took my offer. She didn't want to live in rural Wyoming with me. I understood that, because Portia didn't, either. We had quarterly sex. I took care of it when I came to New York on business trips every three months. That should have done it." Cordell shook his head as if he didn't understand the problem. His deep, ragged tone bore a wounded uncertainty that tore at Jillian's soft heart as he said, "My ex-wife used this thing, and my fiancée isn't marrying me. That says a lot about me, doesn't it?"

Cordell mentioned sex as casually as if he were talking about shaking hands over a business deal; Jillian shifted uncomfortably. For an instant, she realized why Alicia might not want to become the "replacement wife." Romance and tenderness did not seem to be Cordell's concern, though clearly he was puzzled and wounded. She noted Cordell's scowl had changed to dull acceptance.

"I'm sorry," she repeated, taking Bomber's box from Cordell's lap. She was very careful not to touch his towel. She didn't want it to slip farther. "You know, virility..." She glanced at Cordell, stripped down to a towel that clung damply to his narrow hips and... He was definitely manly. After a deep breath, she changed her wording. "Sexuality isn't everything."

"Sit down," he offered without real warmth, still staring at the New York skyline. He looked exactly like Rodin's statue *The Thinker*. She wondered if the model was pondering his masculinity and the awesome, intricate nature of a relationship between a man and a woman. Cordell sighed, his burden clearly heavy.

She sensed he needed a friend; she couldn't leave him to face his double tragedy alone. She set Bomber aside on the couch, which was littered with old photographs, noting that one was of a young Cordell and a beautiful bride in an elaborate, expensive wedding dress. He wore a gray Stetson and a western cut suit and was beaming down at his bride. Cordell shook his head slowly, and Jillian struggled for the right thing to say. "Ah... I find that at times like this, a cup of tea helps," she said finally. Cordell didn't answer; he was clearly in a daze. "I'll make some, if you like."

Cordell, wrapped in his agony and his slipping towel, held the device and the curled message. Jillian noted the expensive carry-on luggage, a black Stetson tossed on top of a worn, stuffed briefcase, and a path of discarded male clothing leading to the bathroom. She nudged aside the long, rumpled leg of his worn denim jeans and prodded him: "Tea?"

"You know that this adds up to a total strikeout," he said dully.

"Hmm? What was that you said?" she asked, looking away from the damp towel molding the firm line of his thighs.

"Why would a woman use one of these things?" he asked in a slow, sincere tone, turning to her. She sensed a deep wound to his masculinity.

She shivered, uncomfortable with this intimacy. She'd never been a guru of sexual needs. Marsh, her ex-husband, had made that all too clear. "Well...uh...some women believe there is a certain therapy in it."

Cordell snorted in disbelief, the muscle in his jaw contracting. He turned to look out at the window. Jillian thought he looked like a lonely, battered wolf in his kingdom. Her instincts to nurture and heal surged instantly. She realized that he was probably remembering his sexual moments with his wife. She felt like a third party.

"I didn't think Portia was highly sexed. I thought we were more like friends and had a good working relationship. I thought we were happy. Sex seemed . . . passable. I'd fly into town and we'd . . ." He glanced at Jillian, as if remembering her presence, then glowered at the device. "And after that we'd catch up on business. I had my secretary fax her every week. Now I find this."

He inhaled slowly, his burden obviously heavy, and Jillian ached to comfort him. Though she did not care for his marriage-as-business view of things, she had once been discarded herself. "You shouldn't take it so hard," she murmured cautiously.

"Sure," he said listlessly, and Jillian hoped he wasn't planning anything rash. She'd set out to eat the fast food of every nation when she discovered Marsh's infidelity; after her eating marathon, the hospital emergency ward had lacked a certain warmth. As a final humiliation, she'd had to clean a mountain of food wrappers from her car.

Cordell sighed heavily, stared at Alicia's note and shook his head. "There go my best accounts. Alicia had cultivated the president of a top firm. He likes to do business with married people. He'll be at the rehearsal party and the church. Alicia said he liked church weddings and anything to do with romance and hearts. I gave her a necklace once, and she cried. I never knew why."

Jillian glanced around the apartment and found no evidence of a woman inhabitant. The expensively furnished rooms looked sterile, and were cluttered with boxes.

A man knocked on the door and glanced at Cordell, then surveyed the clutter. "Don't forget—the new owners are moving in less than two hours from now, Mr. Dougald. You'll be out by then, right?" he asked hopefully.

Cordell's black, stormy eyes locked on the man who straightened, paled and swept past the door. "My lease is up," Cordell muttered. "I was going to move in with Alicia."

"Where will you go?" asked Jillian, instantly alarmed. Clearly heartbroken, Cordell was now homeless, too.

"Anywhere. I've got to get my things out and make an appearance at the rehearsal tonight. Alicia said the reception later was good for business...a Saturday-night mingle-party thing. I'll go to the church tomorrow. Alicia wants me to take care of the caterers and ask the guests to take back their gifts. She's not available. I've got a few hours to fill, meanwhile.... I need a drink," Cordell muttered, rising suddenly in a lithe movement that startled Jillian. He slapped his Stetson on the back of his head. In automatic, efficient movements, he drew on his socks and boots. He padded toward a gleaming bar, armed with the symbols of his rejection—the pigeon and the feminine appliance.

He slammed them on the bar. "The wedding Alicia wanted has cost a fortune. I bought a damn tux, and the reception alone will bankrupt me. I hate those things, anyway. But both Portia and Alicia wanted me to practice business-social skills."

"Maybe you could salvage something," Jillian offered. Cordell would be dynamite in a tuxedo. Dressed in his hat, boots and a towel, he could sell anything. "What about the champagne? No, not champagne." She feared he would drink too much to dull his pain. "Stuffed mushrooms?"

"Fungus," he muttered, jerking open a well-stocked liquor cabinet. "Mushrooms are fungus." He splashed a dark potent-looking liquid into a thick glass, and studied its amber depths. "God, I hate fungus. No matter how many shrimp you stuff in them, they're still fungus. You know where they grow, don't you? Rotted logs and manure."

"Drinking will not cure your heartache, Cordell," Jillian stated firmly. She'd decided that Cordell knew more about botany than he did romance. She'd never feel the same way about mushrooms again. "You can cry if you want to. Tears do help."

"Women." He bit off the word and leveled a scowl at her. "Look, lady—it's been a hell of a day, okay? Why don't you just run along?"

He wasn't asking a question; he was demanding that she leave. But she couldn't leave him awash in his pain.

"You're coming with me," she said firmly, and faced him. Despite his rather clinical views of marriage, Cordell was homeless and he'd been dumped at the altar. His pet, shared with his former love, was deceased—murdered by Atlas. Jillian wouldn't forgive herself if she deserted Cordell now. "I will not allow you to wallow in a pit of misery."

"Uh." The grunt carried his disbelief. He studied her slowly, sizing up her five-foot-eight-inch height and her rounded body. "You and who else is going to keep me from it?" he asked challengingly.

She didn't like his tone, or the challenging lift of his black eyebrow. "Don't argue with me, Cordell. I know misery when I see it. Your heart is breaking. You're coming with me. I'll see you through this. You'll pack your boxes in my van and help me at the food kitchen. While we're working, feeding the needy, we'll discuss your romance with Alicia. Maybe she just has bridal jitters and you can woo her before the ceremony tomorrow. That would be very romantic."

Jillian stood very still, then leaped into her next thought. "I'll coach you. Maybe you could talk her into eloping. That's romantic, and will serve the same purpose. I think if we work hard enough, we can salvage your wedding. What you need to do is to get into your feminine side. Explore your sensitivity and shower Alicia with intimacy and caring. A fax won't do this time, Cordell," she finished firmly. "Have you been listening? Listening and picking up the signals on how she feels? Did you work on your friendship with her? How good are you at intimacy and fantasies?"

"Intimacy. Fantasies. Friendship?" he repeated slowly, his black eyes lashing out at her. "Listen, you little do-gooder, I do not have a feminine side," he stated belligerently between his teeth.

His pride wouldn't allow him to approach his reluctant bride. The wound was too new. Also, he clearly considered the notion that he might have a feminine side a mark against his masculinity.

"I'll be there for you," Jillian replied firmly, patting his hand. She sensed an alert stillness in him, and the shadows around him seemed to shift. He looked at her as though seeing her for the first time. She glanced at the shoe box. "Along the way to the food kitchen, do you suppose we could bury Bomber in the park, near the daffodils?"

Cordell studied the intruder wearing Nanna Bear's Honey Design. Around thirty years old, the woman had frothy, waving blond hair that spilled to her shoulders, and a peaches-and-cream complexion that was perfect for the denim-and-lace design.

The tiny mole beneath the right side of her mouth was the only irregularity in her face. Her jaw was slightly rounded, and above an average nose were two worried, widely spaced green eyes tilting up at the corners. She wore no cosmetics, and her light brown brows had a solid look, winging up before her temples. His gaze skimmed from the clean cut of her cheekbones to her ears, which were dimpled with small pearl studs, then back to her mouth and that saucy little mole.

While Alicia and Portia dressed in simple, expensive business suits, with fashionable haircuts and tall, model-thin bodies, Jillian had the soft, warm look of an old-fashioned girl. She was perfect for his Nanna Bear designs. She had the cuddly look of a woman a man could snuggle up next to—he knew instinctively that her breasts would fit perfectly into his hands. He'd studied models' bra sizes when he designed the Honey vest, and decided to use a princess cut to allow for a bustier woman; Jillian was probably a 34C bra size.

"I asked you if I had any sex appeal," he repeated slowly, surprised to find that he had been focused on her.

"You have two distinct eyebrows, and no hair on your shoulders," she replied instantly.

Cordell gripped the counter of the bar. His whiskey comfort, the dead bird and the damning appliance were all forgotten. "What does that mean?" he asked warily.

It was her turn to look away to the New York horizon studded with jutting concrete buildings. Her flush fascinated him. It started at her throat and worked its way slowly upward. He wondered if her mole got warm.

"I...I wouldn't know," she said stiffly. Then she turned to him and said firmly, "I do know that you need a friend now, and for the moment I want to help, but I'm scheduled to work at the homeless food kitchen—"

As he passed her on his way to his carry-on luggage, Cordell noted the woman's flowery scent. It was a perfect match for the Honey line.

Dear heart... The words whispered through his mind. He stopped in midstride, remembering the tenderness of the tone of his father's voice. The deep voice had leaped at him across thirty years; Cordell shook his head, pushing aside the jolt of pain. He picked up his shaving kit and walked toward the bathroom. He didn't want to go into the bedroom again. He wondered where Portia had used her little friend. He sidestepped the couch.

"Where are you going, Cordell?" Jillian asked worriedly, at his side. She touched his arm. "You, ah...you wouldn't do anything rash, would you?"

Cordell stood in front of the bathroom mirror and studied the woman gripping his arm with both her hands. She looked up worriedly at him. "Who are you?" he asked, considering the pale fingers locked on his darker flesh. He flexed his forearm lightly, and she jerked her fingers away.

Alarm sprang into her green eyes, and a gleaming tendril of hair danced near her glasses. She blew it away. "Oh! I am so sorry. I didn't introduce myself. I, uh...was a little off balance when you opened the door," she returned urgently. "I'm Jillian Horton."

Cordell ran the Horton account through his memory and decided that nothing so soft and caring could be related to the Horton family. The Hortons were tall, dark, angular, and as warm as frozen steel. He lifted the straight razor out of his shaving kit, preparing to shave, a familiar, male ritual that was comforting in his unsteady emotional state.

For a moment, he looked at his grim expression in the mirror. "Whatever happened to good old-fashioned sex?" he asked, still bemused by his recent discovery. "You know, the thing a teenage boy dreams about and can't wait for?"

Clearly alarmed, Jillian stared at the razor's gleaming blade. She gripped his wrists. "You wouldn't. I won't let you."

"How are you going to stop me?" he asked blankly, wondering why she didn't want him to shave.

"Oh, please! Please don't!" she cried, and launched herself into his arms, holding him tightly and pressing her cheek against his chest.

Cordell stood very still, aware of a softness he'd never known before. Scents of spring flowers floated from her, with an earthier woman aroma. He was very aware of the soft pressure of her breasts and her thighs. His senses told him to hold very still; they told him that this soft creature could give him comfort and ease. In the fern-laden bathroom, she reminded him of a woodland nymph. One he would like to capture and bear away into his cave. He knew instinctively that he wanted to fill her, to watch her expression as he made love to her. He blew away a wispy tendril from his cheek and another from his nose. Then he placed the razor on the countertop and gently folded his arms around the soft, curved body of the woman hugging him desperately. "I won't," he whispered, inhaling the flowery scents of her hair.

Dear heart, I knew when I saw you that you were the only woman for me... Cordell remembered the tenderness with which his father had embraced his mother. He frowned over the top of the woman's frothy, silky hair. Why were these memories coming back after years of being locked away?

"You need counseling," Jillian whispered desperately. "You have to recognize and deal with your feminine side, that's all. A little hug here, a tender kiss there. Try nurturing something. A plant, maybe. Oh, Cordell, if you would just allow yourself to cry..."

He nuzzled her fragrant, silky hair and studied the lights there as his fingers eased through the strands. He gently pressed his open hand against her back, easing her breasts against him.

She fit him perfectly standing up; at the moment, he'd prefer her lying beneath him. He wondered about lifting her to the countertop... He stiffened slightly as he remembered Portia's love of automation, and decided that sex in the bathroom was out.

"You're coming with me," Jillian said firmly beneath his chin. "I wouldn't forgive myself if anything happened to you. We'll move your things into my van—you don't appear to have very much—then you can help me at the food kitchen, and then I'll go to the reception and then I'll take you home with me. I'll go to the church with you on Sunday. I'll take care of you.''

"I'm not turning up at the church. So you see me as an orphan?'' he asked slowly, closing his eyes. He'd been an orphan until Nanna yanked him out of the children's home. He'd already lost a mother, father and a baby sister in a plane crash, and he'd decided never to open his heart again. Nanna had been bullying the orphanage administrator when she saw him run by, already out of control. A savage, the administrator had called him. That had been the first time Nanna lassoed him; it hadn't been the last.

A bit of the savage lurked within him now, the highly sexual need to plant himself deeply within this woman. Jillian looked up at him with trust. Sunlight danced off the tips of her lashes as she said, "Cordell, you shouldn't be left alone now. Not with Bomber and Alicia and—''

"If you let me shave first, I'll come with you," Cordell heard himself offer slowly. With his world in pieces and the past preying on his mind, he might as well allow himself to be adopted. Temporarily. Just until he was up to dealing with his current calamities.

Mmm...how I love a man with a clean shave, his mother whispered in a flirtatious tone down through the years. Cordell saw his fingers shake. The long hours of work and travel were getting to him.

"Shave?" Jillian asked in alarm, then glanced down at his straight razor. She stepped back, out of his arms, and Cordell missed her soft, curved warmth as she straightened her clothing with shaking hands. Again the rush of pink surged up to touch her cheeks. "Oh! Oh, I see. That's an old-fashioned razor, isn't it? You weren't going to—''

"No. I'm an old-fashioned guy with a heavy beard. Are you married?" he asked, hoping she wasn't.

She relaxed slightly and smoothed her vest. He didn't tell her that a button had opened and from his height he could see the neat crevice between her breasts. Her peach lace bra lifted and fell rapidly with each breath. Tiny freckles dusted her skin like gold dust. Cordell had always liked panning for gold.

"I was married," she answered crisply. "It didn't work out."

"What happened?" He wondered why any man would let this soft, caring creature escape him. She reminded him of a gentle-eyed doe in a meadow. Except for that enticing, slightly wicked chocolate-drop mole near her mouth.

"Well, apparently I'm not up to par as a wife," she said after looking down at her laced hands. "I like bottling in the catsup factory. I'm not into upward mobility, and I'm not good at marriage."

"Neither am I," he murmured, wanting to bury his face in the cloud of her golden hair.

"Oh..." She lifted her gaze to study his face; then she lifted her hand to place it along his jaw. "Don't think that you aren't. While I know what my problems are, you might need only minor realignment...."

2

He trapped her hand with his, resisting her attempt to draw away. "Realignment?" he asked, frowning down at her.

"Don't bully me, please," she asked in a precise and delicate but firm tone. He reluctantly let her fingers slip from his; they were soft, fragile and enticing. He wanted them on him, anywhere, but this woman was pushing him.

"What's this damn business about realigning my thinking?" he demanded harshly. "I'm the one who has been dumped."

"Could we talk about this later?" she asked.

"I think fine," he said flatly after rummaging through his mental processes. He'd worked to find the right wife, the right expensive accessory for his business.

Jillian smiled consolingly. "Of course you do, Cordell. You're just too emotional right now to be logical."

"Too emotional? I'm not logical?" he repeated in a soft bellow. He was unused to anyone criticizing him on a personal level. "Look, lady...I...am...not...an emotional man. *My* ducks are in a row, and you've got weird ideas."

"We'll talk later," she murmured sympathetically, slipping out of the bathroom and leaving him with the scent of her perfume. He absently noted the soft sway of her hips and the enticing way the bias-cut Honey skirt caressed her calves. Over her shoulder, she said, "You shave, and I'll start carrying boxes out to my van. Don't worry. My friends say I'm a rock when the going gets tough. I'm due now at the food kitchen. We can talk while we work, and never fear, I'll stick with you through your ordeal. You won't face the crowd of well-wishers alone. You can count on me, Cordell. You're traumatized now, unable to release emotions that are eating at you. I will take care of you."

Cordell stared at her as she lifted a box. "No one takes me on as a charity case," he muttered, recognizing a sudden loneliness surging through him. He really wanted to hold this Jillian-woman close to him.

Dear heart, his father had called his mother. . . .

He studied the rounded shape of her bottom as she bent, and wondered how her hips would fill his hands.

Cordell closed his eyes against the sudden sexual urge buffeting him, and knew that before the night was over, he'd try to get the woman into his bed. Troubled by the memory of his father's voice, Cordell realized that he was overtired and susceptible to memories he didn't want. He was an old-fashioned man, and always had been, and he'd been celibate for a long time. However, his instincts told him that loving this woman would temporarily soothe the restlessness within him. He glanced at her breasts, propped on the box beneath them—and was unprepared for the jolt of sexual desire hardening his body.

Cordell stroked his unshaven jaw and wondered when he had last wanted a woman so desperately. He remembered that he'd never rolled in a meadow of flowers or made love in the sunlight. He'd never sipped champagne from a woman's navel or tasted one intimately. And he desperately wanted to trail his lips over her breasts' freckles.

Jillian looked up and straight at him. Her eyes were soft and tender and misty. Cordell felt a strange flip-flop in the area of his heart and decided that the airline breakfast had caused heartburn. Jillian smiled slightly, her expression understanding and compassionate. "I will take care of you, Cordell."

"Yes, boss. Yes, whatever you say," Cordell muttered as he stood beside Jillian, serving food to the homeless and needy.

"Don't slam the mashed potatoes onto their plates," Jillian repeated in a low command. "They are not responsible for your problems. Try a smile, big guy," she urged, grinning up at him.

Cordell scowled down at her, forced his lips to draw back from his teeth and plopped potatoes onto the next plate with a chef's flourish. The X. Fashion Plate account was gone; he'd counted on that last heavy order to finance his catalog and television advertising plan. The Horton chain would never have exclusive retail rights to Nanna Bear... Jillian's breast brushed his arm as she reached to place baked beans on a patron's plate. He stopped thinking about dead accounts and focused on the sudden hardening of his body.

She nodded. "Much better. See? You can learn. By the way, did you compliment either Alicia or Portia? Did you tell them you loved them? Frequently?"

"No. There wasn't a need for that." Cordell stood very still while she moved around to his back and tightened his apron. Behind him, she whispered, "These people need hugs, not scowls, with their meals, Cordell. Try nurturing. You were wonderful with that little boy and his broken toy car. You should have seen your face while you changed that diaper. It looked like you were using your creative ability to the fullest.''

Then her arms went around him, and she hugged him briefly before returning to his side. She smiled at a wrinkled bag lady with a pucker where her teeth should be. "See? A hug a day helps the weary heart."

He inhaled, picking through the turkey-and-dressing scents to find her flowery ones. He wanted to pick Jillian up in his arms and run to the nearest shadowy corner and kiss the sweet curve of her lips. His body leaped every time she ladled green beans and brushed against him.

Jillian was very, very soft. She had cried over Bomber's grave. Cordell had almost plucked her into his arms and sat with her in his lap. The thought jolted him. He couldn't remember Alicia or Portia sitting on his lap. He couldn't remember wanting to cuddle their bony butts.

Cordell slammed another spoonful of potatoes onto an old man's plate, and Jillian glanced at him anxiously. Then she murmured, "You've had a bad day. You're allowed, I suppose. Just try to contain your grief until we're done, if you can. Let's talk about Alicia and how you can romance her back as your bride. By the way, what business are you in?"

"I'm self-employed, and I do not wish to recover Alicia," Cordell stated. He didn't want Jillian to know she was wearing his design. Few people knew that he actually designed the crocheted-lace-and-denim outfits; they thought his grandmother had. Nanna couldn't cook or design. She was a crusty Wyoming rancher who knew about harsh weather, crops, horses and breeding stock. She considered fashion jeans with lace at the cuffs to be "sissified."

Cordell preferred the public notion that a woman designed the feminine clothes. The male designers he noted wore ponytails and flowing clothing, like silk. Give him denim any day.

"You're wounded now. Your heart is broken. But 'recover' sounds like fixing a business loss. A relationship is not a business, Cordell. You must work on getting in touch with your emotions..." Jillian paused when Cordell looked down at her, eyes narrowed with thoughts of how he'd like to get very emotional—the heart-throbbing, mind-blasting, cuddling, steamy, sucking-kissing sort of emotional—with her.

She nervously licked her lips, and he wanted to taste them, to nibble on their softness and to taste her tongue with his. He wanted to wrap himself in her softness and make love to her, the old-fashioned way. Her hand fluttered to cover the gold heart on her necklace. "Anger will not solve anything, Cordell," she stated primly.

He smiled coldly at her, pushing away the fantasy of exploding within her. "Lady, face a waiting crowd at an expensive reception, tell them you've been dumped like old meat, lose business accounts, and then tell me not to be a little—just a tad—miffed," he replied. He was using words he had heard Jillian say earlier.

"You are not old meat, Cordell," she said, and blew a damp, clinging tendril from her temple. "Don't think for a moment that you are past your prime as a man."

"My ex-wife used a—" He could not bear to identify the plastic interloper. "My to-be bride doesn't want me. That says a lot about a man's life. *Which* is in the toilet, lady," he snapped, then added, "I need a good stiff drink."

You are not turning to drink when times are tough, Ward, his mother's voice whispered. *Turn to me.* Cordell swallowed quickly, shaken by the memory of his father grieving over his mother's rough hands. He wrenched himself away from the memory, shaken by it. He didn't want to remember anything of his parents; the pain was too great.

Jillian's eyebrows lifted as she unwrapped her apron and hung it on a hook. "Cordell, trust me. I will be at your side. Unless you have a friend you want to call . . . you really should have someone to tell your problems to, especially tonight."

"I had hoped for a wife," he returned bleakly, as she began undoing his apron knot. He heard himself say, "Hug me again, Jillian."

She hesitated for only a moment, and in that moment, Cordell knew that he needed her.

He hadn't needed, really needed, anyone since his parents and baby sister had died in the plane crash. The thought shocked him. He went very stiff as Jillian caught him to her, her arms locked around his waist. Her wispy, silky cloud of hair settled around his chin and jaw, and Cordell's tension eased. He tightened his arms around her. "Thanks," he said roughly, to cover his shaken emotions.

She stepped back and beamed up at him. "See? Aren't hugs marvelous? My, that scowl you're wearing is suspicious." She glanced at an elderly woman who had clearly been crying, and rushed to her. With her arm around the woman, Jillian listened intently to her. The woman spoke brokenly, wiping her eyes with a balled-up handkerchief. Jillian's expression slid from concern to frustration to anger. She glanced at Cordell. "She's been taken by that scam artist. Squirrels—that's his name—preys on the elderly, taking their life savings. I've just got time to run him down before your reception—uh, before going with you. He's not getting away with this again.''

"I'll go with you," Cordell said, more comfortable with hunting a criminal than with facing his need for Jillian. Or with the memories tugging at him after years of peace.

"You're too emotional now, Cordell. You could get hurt," Jillian said worriedly. "I'll come back for you."

"Where is that little weasel?" Cordell asked. Punching out a scam artist might salve his disastrous day.

Jillian told him the address, and Cordell recognized the rough neighborhood. "You'll take care of me," he said smoothly, disgusted by predators who snatched the savings of the elderly and needy. "Let's go."

"I saw you give money to people at the food kitchen. Annie and Elmer will love their new false teeth. Telling her to send the bill to you was so very nice of you, Cordell," Jillian stated as she drove her van onto the trash-littered street. "You are a nice man, really. A regular good guy. You just don't seem to have the knack of relationships. Don't glower at me. I don't scare easily, and you need me." Rap music seemed to be coming from every boarded window, and graffiti marking a gang's territory was scrawled on the bricks. Jillian knew the leader of the gang, and he was a very nice boy.

"This is the address." Cordell slid from the van before it was fully stopped. Dressed in a black sweatshirt, worn and faded jeans and expensive boots, he looked very tough and lean. The Stetson low on his head added another dimension. He looked as though nothing—not tornadoes, blizzards or war—could keep him from rooting out the man he wanted. He resembled John Wayne and Dirty Harry. Jillian shivered a bit and understood a bit of Alicia's qualms. Cordell could be a formidable opponent as a marriage partner. A man of determination and action, Cordell could change a little tiff into a hazardous zone.

He had a raw energy that frightened her—*and he'd make a wonderful father.*

The second thought just plopped into her mind and nestled there; she remembered how gently Cordell had held the babies and the other children at the shelter. She remembered his concern for each child, and the way he'd listened to them. Cordell had all the makings of a wonderful father—just the sort of man she'd always wanted to father her children, adopted or natural. Jillian gasped and shook her head; she must be light-headed because of lost sleep and having skipped breakfast.

Marsh had destroyed romantic ideas of marriage and motherhood for her. The submissive-little-wifey role had been painful, especially once Marsh found her insecurities and preyed cruelly upon them. An undercooked potato was a disaster; his shoes not being polished or left in a line was a criminal offense. He'd dismissed her talent for marketing as a momentary flash in the pan. "You couldn't do it again," he'd said. "You can't even make tapioca pudding without a mess."

She couldn't see Cordell starting a world war because his shirts were pressed wrong. Cordell's jeans were familiar and worn, and his sweatshirt was even a bit tattered.

She put Marsh and his mental abuse behind her. She preferred to remember his silly, stunned expression after she'd dumped a bowl of tapioca over his head. *It* created a lumpy separation of his eyebrows. That had been when she discovered his part in a charity scam. From that heartbeat on, she had determined never again to be the downtrodden little wifey without brains.

Jillian just had time to pay a teenager to watch her van and promise more if it remained safe before Cordell entered the building. She ran up the stairs and followed Cordell's long stride down the littered, dirty hallway. She grabbed his arm, but he shrugged her off easily. She clutched him again, hugging his arm to her breasts as he dragged her along. "I'll handle this, Cordell. I'm very good at getting what I want."

"So am I," he said tightly. That instant, he turned his attention to her. Her senses tingled, and the hair on the nape of her neck rose. The light in his black, narrowed eyes was definitely hot and predatory. "I always get what I want."

Out of kindness, she chose not to remind him of Alicia and Portia. He rapped on the scarred door, and Jillian pressed herself in front of him. She knocked delicately. "Anyone home?"

Cordell lifted her aside, turned the doorknob and walked into the room. Squirrels Johnson tried to run past him. Cordell caught the young man by his collar and hauled him upright. Squirrels, younger and thinner than Cordell, looked like a child, his feet dangling four inches above the ground.

"Listen, you little punk. I don't have time to sweet-talk you. I am not in a good mood. I'm supposed to be a groom tomorrow, but I won't be. This does not make me happy. Today, you are to give money back to the old woman you just scammed. Then you are to work in the food kitchen whenever you have free time—if you don't have free time, make it. And you are to send me progress reports every week at this address." He tucked a business card into Squirrels' jacket, lowered the boy to the floor and waited while the youth stuttered about his innocence.

"Uh-huh," Cordell said in a satisfied tone after a moment. Then he glanced at Jillian, who had just placed a restraining hand on his arm. "Oh, yeah. The hug," he muttered. "Today I'm into nurturing, kid. Trust me, it's a real bargain—not offered every day. Do we have an agreement or not?"

Squirrels shook and nodded, clearly frightened. Cordell inhaled briefly, then bent to hug the youth. Squirrels turned pale and shivered, his eyes wide with panic, as his toes left the ground. Cordell dropped him, stepped back and smiled grimly. "So we have an agreement?"

Squirrels nodded again, and Cordell reached out to shake his hand. The youth's tremulous smile was more of a painful wince as Cordell nodded. "Good. Because if you don't follow my outline, son, I'll be back, and I'm worse than Dirty Harry when I'm mad. Got it?"

An hour later, Jillian was pulling her van out of a Mexican-food drive-through. Around her burrito, she muttered, "Dirty Harry. That was some tough-guy act. But you spoiled it by offering to let him come to your ranch if he reformed."

Cordell watched her with interest, and glanced back at the cartons of Chinese food she had previously purchased. He helped himself to the hot dog she had just bought from a street vendor. The empty cartons in the back of her van rolled and rattled at each swerve to the next food stand. He studied her scowl—it was cute. A soft, feminine frown that a man could probably kiss and soothe away. Cordell wanted to do that now. "You're mad," he stated sagely.

"That's one way of putting it," Jillian returned as she honked at the next traffic jam. "You scared Squirrels."

Cordell reached to tuck a napkin into the top of her blouse. She recognized the gesture as an offering to make peace. "I like that outfit."

"I know how to handle problems like this, Cordell," she muttered as he studied her closely. She ripped away the napkin and crushed it. "I never threaten. I use reason."

"You'd never use an appliance like Portia's. You're one hot woman," he stated slowly, firmly.

"You're right." She leveled her best killer glare at him. His remark concerning her growing temper was true. "I'm very angry with you. Though the hug showed real progress," she added, to soften the blow. Cordell did not need her anger added to his doubly disappointing day.

Jillian munched on her beefless burrito. "You looked like some western bounty hunter, taking those steps two at a time—"

She choked and sputtered. Cordell was honorable even in his anger. He had a tender heart. He was considerate of the elderly and needy. At the kitchen, he had held and played with children, clearly enjoying himself. Beneath Cordell's tough exterior lurked a playful boy and a caring man.

A man she could love. But she'd given her heart before, and she wouldn't again. . . .

Jillian inhaled Cordell's fresh, woodsy scent, and her heart quivered as she caught a deeper, more manly scent, mixed with it. Her feminine antennae latched on to that slightly musky, exciting aroma. She hadn't had many heart quivers in her life, and perhaps she was getting emotionally involved with a man who was in her care. She soared to the side of the street and quickly purchased a meatless taco from a street vendor. While Cordell watched with interest, she finished it quickly. Then she drove through the shaded street to her small apartment building and parked the van. She stared at children playing ball in the street, and at Mrs. Jones, who was sweeping the sidewalk. Jillian shook her head. She had definitely been off balance from the moment Cordell opened the door wearing a towel and holding Portia's appliance.

For a woman who had taken the reins of her life in hand, steered the course of her ship and the ships of other people, Jillian found Cordell a problem.

The burrito, the taco, the fried Chinese noodles and the chicken hot dog she'd eaten began to churn in her stomach. Cordell had looked godlike, an Adonis, wearing that towel as no other man could. She loved the neat space between his black brows and the smooth, hairless gleam of his shoulders, and his flat, muscular stomach.

She realized belatedly that Cordell had sat nearer and placed his arm around her. "You need a hug," he murmured before bending to kiss her lips lightly. He moved quickly, sliding out of the van and coming around to open her door.

Jillian, still wrapped in the light, tender kiss, led him into her small, cluttered apartment. She reasoned that the kiss was because Cordell was trying to get in touch with his gentler side. After all, he'd already hugged Squirrels.

Cordell carried his expensive garment bag as he walked around the one room, studying the open, rumpled sofa bed. He looked big, bold and masculine in her brightly colored ruffles-and-lace apartment. From the closed window, Atlas watched the new male entering his domain with a territorial eye. "This is it. If we're going to make the reception, you'd better move it," Jillian said briskly to conceal her tumbling emotions.

He stared grimly at her bed, and the long, frothy pink rosebud nightgown draped across it. His black eyes found Jillian's and locked on to her. His lowered lashes did not conceal his smoldering gaze. Her body began to throb. She wondered when flames would spring into the room. The immediate, hard tightness deep within her body shocked her. She felt juicy, hot and ripe.

The room hummed with tension. Cordell filled the space, making it too warm and close. She tried to breathe, and sucked in a heady whiff of his male aroma. The juicy-ripe sensation lurched and swelled. "Move it," she managed, as Cordell's gaze traced her lips.

At six feet three inches, he had a lot to move. Cordell nodded and found the bathroom. She hurriedly made and folded the sofa bed, ate a carton of cold fried Chinese noodles and chewed an antacid tablet. Cordell emerged minutes later with a bath towel around his hips. He had shaved again, and the towel's cabbage-rose print enhanced his masculinity. "Your turn."

Jillian sailed by him, carrying her basic-black dress and the shreds of her emotions. For just a moment, she sensed that Cordell wanted to pick her up in his arms and carry her to the sofa bed. She closed the tiny bathroom's door and wondered why she'd never replaced the lock. She inhaled Cordell's freshly bathed scent and studied his opened shaving kit. The male toiletry items mocked her in the feminine flower-and-ruffles bathroom.

She froze when she saw the folded bundle of condoms. They glittered in foil packages, not the superstud variety, but the practical kind. Cordell was a prepared, well-stocked groom. That amount of prevention would frighten any woman. Its implications exceeded what Marsh had said was the American national average.

Jillian shivered. If Cordell wanted her now, it was because he was on the rebound. For her part, she was supersensitized by guilt and compassion.

None of that explained why she wanted Cordell to pick her up in his arms. Why she wanted him to kiss her. Why she wanted to lock both arms around him and keep him safe. And why she wanted to kiss each line around his mouth and his eyes, and the one separating his eyebrows. She wanted to kiss his hairless shoulders and the nipple that had jumped when he gripped that sexual tool...

Jillian breathed rapidly, rested her back against the door and groaned lightly. At that moment, she wanted Cordell with a passion that shocked her. Until Cordell, her passions had run to fast foods when she was upset.

She firmed her lips and stepped into the shower. Cordell's after-shave stood beside her bath gel. His straight razor rested on a shelf with her exfoliant body scrub and blue mud mask.

Jillian let the hot water stream through her hair and down her body. She balled her fists and groaned, fighting the thought of Cordell making love to her. Of her loving Cordell as he should be loved. Of herself wearing a bridal veil and pledging her love to him.

Because he fit her. While she lectured him about scaring Squirrels, his larger hand had slid exactly into hers. The fit of their palms and their intertwined fingers had been perfect, his thumb protectively on the outside of hers and his larger pinkie nestled intimately within her keeping. When she hugged him, she'd sensed a solid man who would stay when life's hurricanes thrashed them. She'd sensed a gentle man when he bent to give a homeless girl money for hair ribbons. "Oh, Cordell," she whispered hopelessly into the water spray. She didn't want the emotions rising in her. She balanced her past with Marsh against a future with Cordell—and she wanted him in her life. She wanted to explore him further. Attuned as she was to advertising, Jillian knew that timing was everything. Cordell was leaving town, and she had to nab him while she could ... "Oh, what am I doing?"

Jillian scrubbed her hair and body vigorously, trying to dislodge the whimsical thought. It returned when she dried her hair and felt, somehow, like a bride on her wedding night. She was tense, emotional and overtired. Her fatigue was probably due to the strain of the people she was emotionally supporting—like Jessica, who didn't understand regular work hours and why people demanded so much of her. Like Petey, who couldn't balance his checkbook.

Jillian shivered again. She definitely felt the way she imagined a bride might feel. Or a woman about to step over a dangerous cliff.

In his dress shirt and slacks, Cordell lounged on the folded sofa bed and wondered how he could trap Jillian. He wallowed in her scents. He surveyed her homey, cluttered apartment and listened to the multiple taped messages. Everyone needed something from Jillian. She was a fixer, a soother, and she had a host of Cling-ons burdening her with their problems. The quiet anger in Cordell built each time Jessica called, seeking refuge from work.

Nora wanted a married man, but not like the last married man. Nora was certain this married man, as opposed to the last five, would leave his wife for her. Tom wanted to borrow five hundred to see him over until he won his next demolition derby; Joe wanted Jillian to baby-sit his kids because he wanted to go to a party on his visitation time. Or rather, four parties. Or he might have a sexy weekend guest and he might need baby-sitting for next week. Lydia needed emotional support—her new "boob job" was lopsided and she was wondering about a tummy tuck. Tom now needed six hundred dollars for living expenses, and Dora wondered if Jillian would take up a half inch in her left slacks leg by tomorrow morning. "Cling-ons," Cordell muttered, wanting desperately to claim Jillian for his own.

He turned the idea of getting her into his bed into something longer-term, perhaps marriage, with exclusive rights and no damned appliances. He wouldn't want to spend every tax quarter alone in his bed if he could have Jillian sharing it. He'd be happy to pay regular installments. He smoothed the long pink rosebud gown slung across the back of the sofa bed. Jillian, blushing and nervous, as she had been in the van and on the way into her apartment, wouldn't need rosebuds to make her adorable.

Cordell drew the nightgown against his cheek, rubbing it and inhaling her scents. He wanted her for his own. He wanted her wearing his ring, in his bed, and in his life. The need was selfish, primitive, and surprised him. He hadn't really cared about Portia or Alicia sharing his life. They hadn't fascinated him with blushes and hugs, soft emotions and curves that made his body leap to arousal at the slightest brush....

Jillian stepped from the bathroom too soon, and his instinctive need to capture her lurched to life. He'd expected her to take the hours necessary for Alicia and Portia, the only women with whom he'd shared brief living arrangements. Nanna's few dress-up occasions took all of ten minutes.

Jillian's short, long-sleeved dress took his breath away as it clung to her, revealing endless long legs. She'd done something saucy with her hair, piled it up high and allowed tendrils to caress the nape of her neck. Cordell blinked. He'd just discovered another cute little mole. Without her glasses and with cosmetics, Jillian's eyes could wrap a man in an instant volcano, and her buttery mauve-tinted lips made a man want to lick and taste them.

Then Cordell spotted the neat cutout in her bodice, framing the tender, pale rise of her breasts. Whatever air was left in his lungs whistled out. His instincts reacted immediately, and he heard himself say, "My grandmother is dying. She's in Wyoming, and her only wish is to see me happily married."

He didn't like himself the moment the false statement was out of his mouth. But when you're in the Cling-on business, you've got to find something that takes top billing, he thought righteously. He wanted all of Jillian's attention, and so he'd lied for the first time since Nanna had washed his mouth with soap at the age of eleven.

While the callers and now himself needed Jillian's touch, he wondered who she needed. He wanted to be that someone. He wanted her to need him.

At the moment, he was having problems with his own needs, which were to claim Jillian and bear her to his bed. The cutout in her tiny black dress could permanently damage him, if he didn't taste her soon. The dainty light dusting of freckles enticed him. He forced himself to breathe, watching her carefully and pushing down his impulse to pluck her up into his arms.

Nanna's false impending death had caused Jillian to stop immediately, allowing Cordell to absorb her, fully primed to accompany him to his reception. A gold heart shone within the cutout bodice. Cordell realized he trembled when he looked at the indentation of her waist and the flare of her hips.

While Jillian was reeling from this new revelation about his misadventures, Cordell slid his hand into hers. She laced their fingers the way he liked, with his pinkie comfortably lodged between her ring and small finger. He wanted his entire body close to hers. He sensed that he would not be complete again until Jillian admitted him into her body. Until he nestled in her warmth and gathered her into his arms without a stitch of clothing between them. His need of her made him uneasy. He wasn't an uneasy sort of guy, but one who knew what he wanted and took it. That was why he'd told Jillian about his "ailing" grandmother, who actually could have armwrestled several young men into submission. He gently tugged Jillian's hand, urging her down toward him.

"Oh, Cordell..." Jillian murmured, in a sympathetic tone that told him he'd scored a hit to her soft heart.

For a second, he hated himself, until those soft hips settled on his lap. Jillian had a lush, womanly feel to her that suited him. He couldn't wait to spread her out beneath him. "I just checked in with her nurse. Grandma just has a few days at the most. She's holding on until she sees my bride. She's in Slough Foot, Wyoming," he added, for a touch of honesty, and wondered fearfully how she felt about the West. His marriage choices had never preferred the rural West. But his instincts were on override, and he was determined to get this soft creature back to his lair.

Jillian's arms enfolded him at once, her hand stroking his hair and the nape of his neck. He eased her closer, and gently settled her head upon his shoulder.

She fit. He slowly settled his cheek alongside her soft one, gently, lightly, and she fit even better. "I've had a bad day," he added softly, nuzzling the soft cloud of fragrant, silky hair enfolding him.

Her hand stroked his nape. "Yes, you have, Cordell. You have had a bad day."

Who cuddled Jillian when she had a bad day? he wondered, and wanted to be that someone.

"I hate to tell Grandma the news," he murmured, running his lips along the curve of her ear. Her arms tightened, just as he'd known they would, and she pressed against him. Cordell slid his hand to her waist and gently inched his way upward until his fingers rested just below her breast.

She fit him perfectly, and for a moment he treasured just holding her in his arms.

Then his instincts told him that nothing would be enough until she was his bride and in his bed and... Cordell realized that he had groaned slightly and that perspiration threatened his upper lip.

"There . . . there . . ." Jillian said soothingly, nestling against him and making his desire for her leap.

Holding her carefully, protectively, Cordell eased her down onto the cushions. She stroked his hair, and those soft, caring eyes of hers darkened as he slowly, slowly lowered his head to her soft, warm breasts. He breathed quietly, listening to her racing heartbeat and acknowledging that it matched his. Her hand continued stroking his nape, soothing him. "I'll see you through this," Jillian murmured unevenly as Cordell nudged the gold heart aside with his lips.

The small cutout in her bodice did not provide the lush warmth he wanted, but for now Cordell didn't trust himself. He'd heard about men wanting women desperately, wanting to take them in a primitive fashion. These men didn't, because they were civilized, though they mourned the lost time as their women made up their minds.

But Cordell's experiences ran to the ones of his youth, the experimental kind, and then the selection of a bride based on business. He eased his hand slowly down the curve of her body. He traced her hipbone with his thumb. He'd never noted that a woman's hipbone could be so interesting, the prelude to her soft belly and the slight mound of her femininity. He'd never considered how a man needed to rest upon feminine hipbones. He left that intriguing line to gently span and lock his fingers upon her hips. His fingertips pressed gently, then dug in slightly, possessively, to test the softness. There was nothing businesslike about the way he wanted Jillian. "I'd better call a motel for a room tonight," he whispered against the warmth exposed by that cutout.

"You'll do nothing of the sort. You'll stay with me," Jillian whispered against his hair. "You're mine to take care of, remember?"

Cordell allowed himself a small smile. He liked being hers to take care of. "You're perfect, Jillian," he said truthfully. But the sensual humming in his body would deepen in the small, intimate apartment. He didn't want to frighten her away into the world of the Cling-ons. "But the motel is a better idea. I...uh...need a bit of space."

"No," she returned firmly. "You'll be lonely and dwell upon your problems. You stay here." Then she treated Cordell to a hug that caused him to harden more.

"Ah . . . by the way," she added breathlessly as he returned the hug, drawing her slightly beneath him and studying her flushed face. He slid his hand beneath her back. He eased her breasts against his chest as she whispered hesitantly, "Ah . . . do you think we could stop somewhere and replace your razor with the electric kind?"

He grunted, too stunned to speak. For in that second he realized that Jillian was not wearing a bra. "Uh . . . did you forget something?" he asked when he could speak, his throat dry.

A man could drown in those dark, soft green eyes. He glanced warily at the cutout, and Jillian tensed immediately. The exposed softness jiggled enticingly, and Cordell feared he would lose control and tell her how much he wanted her, to be buried to the hilt in her sweetness, to be meshed together with her, tighter than a—

If he pushed his needs at her too soon, he would frighten her. Cordell forced himself to sit upright, away from what he wanted most. Jillian's legs were still draped across his lap, and Cordell locked both hands to her thighs, unable to let her go completely. He stared at the cat clock ticking on the wall, the tail swinging back and forth.

At thirty-eight, he'd just discovered that none of his sexual experiences mattered. The need for Jillian was deeper, riveting him to his sofa bed, the fit more right. He sat very still, contemplating this turn and his taut, aching body, and knew that the primitive need for a man to have a certain woman above the rest was true. The revelation shocked him. While Alicia could replace Portia, no one could replace Jillian for him. He'd found what he wanted.

Cordell glanced down at Jillian, who was frowning up at him with a concerned expression. Her frothy blond hair sparkled in the sunlight, spread around her head. Her moist lips trembled and parted and...

Cordell lurched to his feet, slashing his shaking hands through his hair. "Let's go," he said roughly.

3

"When you said that I was a good guy, did you mean it?" Cordell asked on the way to the expensive restaurant. Alicia had combined the business cocktail party, their wedding rehearsal and the dinner into one event because of time. He didn't want to spend too much time in the marrying process. He had allowed five days for a jaunt to New York and marriage.

Jillian ached for him. How he had suffered. She placed her hand on his. When his fingers turned to slide between hers, his palm rough and large against hers, she held him firmly. "You're marvelous. Despite all your wounds today, you've shown love and caring. Even for Squirrels. He's probably never had a man hug him or show interest in his life. You might have changed him for the good. I know that you are a kind, good, caring man."

Cordell looked at their laced fingers. His free hand gripped the overhead handle as she swerved into a tiny parking spot with her van. In the spring twilight, with New York settling noisily around them, the angry blare of horns wiped out a taxi driver's curse and started another man swearing. Jillian smoothed Cordell's gray dress jacket and straightened his western tie as they stood on the pavement. She inspected him from head to toe and smoothed back an errant wave from his ear. He leaned toward her touch, wanting more. "You look good," she said, reassuringly. "Now, remember that whatever happens, I'm here with you. You won't need your Stetson for security. You have me."

"I'll remember," he returned as she reached to smooth his collar. "You're a loyal kind of woman."

"Don't be afraid. You'll rise above this and love again," she whispered.

"Oh, yes," he returned huskily, noting her ability to be supportive. He savored her hands fluttering over his chest, smoothing his jacket. "I plan to."

"This is for the best. Alicia did not deserve you," Jillian stated righteously.

"Uh-huh. Would you mind putting that in writing? I could have a relapse, and might need to remind myself that someone has a high opinion of me," Cordell said softly.

Jillian reached up to touch his cheek. "Yes. Of course. I'll sign something like that."

"Good. I knew you would," he said with certainty. She approved of his smile. It showed confidence. Cordell had asked a small favor to reassure himself with when he was alone. He took a paper from his pocket, placed it on the hood of her van and slashed a note. "I appreciate this, Jillian," he stated huskily. "Here's my pen," he added helpfully.

The neon and the streetlights provided little light to read his black scrawl across the notepad, and Jillian had left her glasses in the van. She noted that his expression was no longer hardened, but rather whimsical. Yet there was a smug air, as if he were getting what he wanted. Like a little boy who had just won all the playing marbles and was running away home with his booty. An endearing little dimple peeped out of his left cheek. His fingertip smoothed the curls at the nape of her neck, and Jillian quivered. She wanted to wrap her arms around him and hug him tightly. She signed her name, and Cordell leaned over her shoulder to inspect the note. His breath warmed her ear and stirred her hair as he murmured, "Good. Would you mind dating it? Just for my personal records? And then there's my grandmother... I hope she lives long enough to read it. She'll be pleased to know that someone cared enough to write it."

"Yes, of course." She dated the note and handed it back to him. In the streetlight, Cordell loomed over her, and the air between them quivered with something she didn't understand. He looked at her very closely, taking in the shape of her face, lingering on her lips. He spent two of her heartbeats studying the mole beside her lips. Her heart leaped when his black gaze lowered and locked hungrily on her breasts.

"You are one fine woman," he whispered, in a tone that shot straight to her senses, swirled around her ears and her throat and locked on to every feminine nerve she possessed. A warm flush started on her skin and began to sink into her breasts, making them peak against the taut fabric. The warmth swirled and lurked and locked on to her lower body, and she experienced a melting that weakened her knees. There was a definite primitive impulse to bear Cordell down to the pavement. Or drag him into the back of her van.

Jillian stepped back, alarmed. She stared up at Cordell, who was looking at her as if he had found what he wanted most. She was unaccustomed to intense study, and suddenly she was very nervous of him. "Ah... are you all right?" she asked.

"Everything is just fine," Cordell returned huskily, his eyes gleaming beneath his lashes. "Just fine."

Cordell's large hand settled at her waist as they walked into the restaurant. He drew her close to him as they entered the expensively decorated room. She allowed him to be very close because she was his support, his strength in a gauche situation—the groom deserted before the wedding.

Her entire family, minus the children, lurked in small groups around the room. She should have known they would not miss an event which starred a popular and potential acquisition—Nanna Bear. Her family always kept very close tabs on social events which might benefit them. They always managed to get invited somehow. Jillian steeled herself for an assault on her clothing, on her actions, on her nowhere life. She moved slightly against Cordell's body, and his arm instantly looped out to draw her closer, protectively. Jillian had rarely been protected or cuddled in her lifetime. The experience, blended with Cordell's clean, masculine scent and his firm body, wasn't that bad.

"What's wrong?" he whispered, bending his cheek close to hers. She had stopped suddenly, and he'd run into her backside. Cordell's long arm had instantly encircled her waist, drawing her back against him. When her bottom touched his body, he groaned achingly, as if in pain. His large hand flattened over her stomach and pressed her tightly against him.

Jillian tensed when her elegant, tall, perfectly groomed parents and sisters turned to her. She realized instantly that Cordell's black head, lowered to hers, revealed a false intimacy, perhaps even a flirtation. She read the instant condemnation of her dress—it was the same one she always wore. Then there was the how-much-do-we-have-to-suffer? look.... "Oh, dear. She never can do anything with that mop of curls. She'll never learn anything about appearing as a member of the Horton family."

She moved closer to Cordell. Though she was used to the thoughtless remarks of her family—they really loved her, and their criticism was well meant—Jillian had to protect this man who had suffered so much in one day. "Ah...Cordell... Do I look all right? My family is here. They must know Alicia. I don't want any reports getting back to her that aren't satisfactory."

His fingers smoothed the curve of her waist, and his little finger rested on the jut of her hip. "Where's your family?"

"The Hortons, of the Horton retail stores. Designer clothing, that sort of thing."

He tensed, glancing around the room and nodding to several people. Jillian held his hand, glad of the way it protectively enfolded her cold one. "Don't worry," she said firmly as her father and mother began their elegant passage toward her. "I'll take care of them for you. Try to smile, Cordell. Let them know that you're on top of your emotions, no matter how badly you're hurting."

George Horton nodded to Cordell and extended his hand. "Good seeing you again, Cordell. I've been looking at your designs. I agree with Alicia that you have a unique product."

Buffy Horton, Jillian's mother, placed her well-manicured hand on George's crooked arm. The family diamonds glittered on her fingers, and a huge emerald-cut diamond rested upon her newly lifted, designer-clad bosom. Tiffany and Jacqueline, equally tall, elegant and dark, appeared with their perfect upper-class husbands. They looked down at Jillian, mocking her.

Her father knew Cordell. The cowboy from Wyoming was looking at her with an unreadable yet wary expression. "Cordell?"

"The up-and-coming owner of Nanna Bear Creations," George stated, in his booming chairman-of-the-board voice.

Jillian turned to Cordell, who gripped her upper arm, not allowing her to move away from him. He looked grim, searching her eyes with his. His jaw shifted from side to side as if he were grinding his teeth; then he lifted his hand for silence in the room. "I have an announcement to make."

"You're Nanna Bear!" Jillian exclaimed, stunned.

"You never wear the right thing, Jillian," Tiffany murmured, smoothing her silk evening dress.

"No wonder your ex-husband hated to go anywhere with you," Jacqueline chimed in elegantly. "Once you changed out of a business suit, you were hopeless. Still are."

"Dear, can't you do something with your hair?" Buffy asked mournfully.

Jillian continued to stare up at Cordell. "You are Mr. Nanna Bear. I love your things," she heard herself say distantly. "Cordell?" she asked, wondering who this man really was, after all.

"Thanks. Lay off her, all of you," Cordell ordered in a low, taut warning tone. He locked his arm around Jillian and pressed her closely, protectively, possessively, to his side.

Buffy's thin eyebrows lifted. "My dear, where is Alicia?"

Cordell grunted and began walking through the crowd to the microphone. Jillian realized belatedly that he was carrying her. Her feet were not touching the floor. She tugged at his jacket, forced to wrap her arm around his back to steady herself.

"Now get this, people. Alicia and I are off. Jillian is marrying me. It's romantic. I won't be at the church tomorrow, so everyone take back anything that's theirs. You might as well go and enjoy the eats. They cost plenty," Cordell stated over the microphone.

Then he grinned down at her, the victor surveying his prey. She stared at his dimple and the reckless black wave crossing his forehead and changed her image of him: the pirate relishing his booty, the boy with his best toy, the groom well warmed and hungry for his bride—

Jillian knew now how Alice in Wonderland felt. Or people dropping in and out of the Twilight Zone. Or an earthperson returning from an experience aboard an alien spaceship.

In a daze, she saw her family blink, reeling with shock. They began wending their elegant way toward her. Her father beamed, and her mother looked almost happy, though careful not to spoil her new facelift. Her sisters were flushed with jealousy as they forced bright smiles at her. Her father strode up to Cordell and shook his free hand. "Good show."

He gave Jillian his seal of approval—a paternal first. "You've finally done something right. Reached out and hooked a big one into the family. Cordell will enhance the Horton retail business by millions. Yes, Jillian, my dear. You've finally done something right," he repeated cheerfully. "Brought home the bacon after all."

Her father leaned closer to whisper, "See if you can get him to sign an exclusive contract with us. If he launches that catalog idea, we'll lose millions. He's thinking about marketing using computer communications."

Buffy bent to whisper in Jillian's ear. "Don't you dare lose this one before you're married. After you get him into the family, your father will tie him up with contracts. Try to get pregnant ASAP—as soon as possible. If he uses prevention, prick holes in them. Children cement marriages, and your father says Cordell is a top talent. Your father wants to go overseas with the Nanna Bear line. He says we'll make a killing and I can have that sweet little villa in Italy."

"Mother!" Jillian took in the envious expressions of her sisters, who had already borne the required cementing children and gone on to have affairs. Jacqueline and Tiffany were looking at Cordell as if they wanted to make him their love slave.

She stared up at Cordell and thought about having his children. About the physical exercise necessary to make a child. About how she wanted to claim him for her own—oh, not like unclaimed baggage, but as a man who suited her, who made her senses leap and who knew how to hold her hand. Her marketing research skills kicked into gear, and she weighed what she knew of Cordell. The chances were good that he could be her perfect fit. The floor slanted oddly beneath her, and only when Cordell's fingertip pushed gently up on her chin did she realize that her mouth was open. He sealed it with a light kiss.

Cordell surveyed the curve of Jillian's hips and neat bottom and hoped that her tiny skirt would ride higher on those impossibly long legs. In her apartment, she'd been striding back and forth in front of him for the past half hour. "You!" was all she had said, but from the dark slashing anger in her eyes, he knew she hadn't uncapped all of her thoughts. Her "You!" was dark, and spelled out a raw anger that would almost have frightened him...if he hadn't been thinking about how passionate she looked, all cute and hot. He wanted to fix everything wrong in her life, like her cold-blooded family talking down to her.

Jillian's hands rested on her waist as she turned to him. Sprawled across her couch, his boot propped on a dainty footstool, Cordell surveyed the long line of her spread legs. "You!" she stated again.

He wondered how a woman so compassionate, so passionate, could have sprung from George Horton's cold loins.

Loins. Cordell's ached and heated each time he looked at Jillian. He wanted to lay her down and sink into her, to lock them together until they were one. She was perfect—feminine, caring, soft—and would be a great mother to their children. He could just see her now, all cute and hot and cuddly and melted around him. As soon as he got her into his life and his bed, all the pieces would settle into place.

Jillian ran her fingers through her hair, the golden cloud spilling around her. Her eyes ignited into green fire; they lashed at him, and Cordell felt the way he had before that mountain cat jumped him. A trickle of uneasiness ran up the back of his neck as she said, very softly, "You had me sign a note saying that I would marry you ASAP."

She crushed the note and hurled it at him. "I won't. You had me mourning over your dead pigeon and your broken engagement...." Jillian came near him. "Cordell, I will not be one of your replacement wives for business purposes. Nor will I be your pawn in your business— By the way, I do adore Nanna Bear designs," she added.

Because she had softened her tirade, Cordell felt obliged to say, "Bomber wasn't mine. He was Alicia's."

"What?" Jillian's eyebrows shot up, and she dashed back a fall of curls from her cheek. "You mean that I was feeling guilty about your bird and it wasn't even *yours?*" she asked, her voice rising indignantly.

He inhaled, realizing that he'd never encountered such a sweet, hot-blooded, hotheaded, passionate woman. In his defense, and because she had just launched a shoe at him, Cordell reasoned, "I did just get dumped. Add that to finding Portia's little toy—"

"There you stood..." She hurled another shoe at him, which he caught, noting that she had cute feet. Slender toes, an arch he'd love to run his fingers across. He imagined her wearing those fuzzy pink house slippers that wives wore when seeing their husbands off to work. She'd look rumpled with sleep, and soft and well loved. Cordell drew a pillow over the pressure against his slacks.

She took a deep breath and began again. "There you stood, a Wyoming cowboy—big as a wall, and wearing a scowl and a towel. You looked as if you'd lost your best friend.... You held that—that thing, and couldn't understand why... Well, skip that part. I felt guilty.... Me, with the cat that killed the bird. Oh, it isn't my cat, of course, more the apartment building's, but Atlas is a friend when things are lonely. You think romance is a... *Whoa...Not romance, but sex on a quarterly basis*...like taxes, right? Hey, guy. I've been through one bloodless marriage. I quit being a doormat and being shoved into corners I didn't like. I am an independent woman, bud," she said, firing each word at him.

She continued to glare at him. "Well, I won't allow myself to be pushed into anything. You just get your two distinct eyebrows and your hairless shoulders out of here."

Though Cordell didn't understand that remark, he knew he had to play his best negotiating point. "Thank you for saving me at the rehearsal-dinner thing. I couldn't have done it without you," he began, trying not to stare at the way her bosom pushed up and down in the cutout as she breathed quickly, angrily. He shifted uncomfortably on the sofa bed, his body taut with all the years of sexual abstinence bottled up and ready to rocket out of him.

"Oh, I'm a real rock, okay," she muttered, reaching to retrieve the crumpled note on the couch beside him. "Give me that note, you bushwhacker. You can't blackmail me into marrying you."

Cordell caught her arm and dragged her into his lap. Very few layers separated him from her. He shivered, controlling her flying hands and his desire to make her his woman.

But he wouldn't, he thought as her elbow struck his eye. He wanted this ill-tempered— She connected with his other eye before he caught her hands. He wanted her to come to him, all soft and sweet and cuddly. Because she fit.

Meanwhile, back in reality, he had her signature on a note promising to marry him. Cordell liked backup plans.

Jillian was staring at him in horror. "Now see what you've made me do. I've never lifted a hand to anyone in anger. I don't even kill insects. Oh, Cordell, you're going to have a black eye!" she cried softly.

Her eyes began to mist, and Cordell's determination turned to jelly. He foraged for something to say to soothe her. But that need warred with the need to claim her, to

make the fit very tight between them. A takeover sometimes required some fast wheeling and dealing. "Two
black eyes," he told her, watching her search his other eye
and mortifying guilt sink into her.

"Oh, dear, oh, dear, oh, dear," she murmured,
touching the slight swelling lightly. "Let me go, Cordell.
I've got to apply first aid...ice packs...steak... Uh, I'm
a chicken-and-fish person...."

"My grandmother used to use ice packs when I came
home all busted up. She took me out of the orphanage,"
he said gently, and watched with fascination as Jillian
swallowed. Her expression said that her caring nature had
overridden her anger. He had to kiss that long, smooth
throat. Gently, while she was busy putting two and four
together, he placed his head upon her shoulder. "Marry
me, Jillian. Come home with me and make Nanna happy
in her last days."

He couldn't desert her, leave her to her family and the
Cling-ons. He wanted to take care of her.

Her tense body softened slightly, and Cordell eased her
closer, his lips against her throat. He found he was rocking her gently, and that she was slowly stroking his hair.
He thought he could spend an eternity just like
this...wrapped up in this woman, treasuring her. He let
the softness settle around him, in him, discovering the
glow rising in him just like a sunrise.

"You deceptive, low-down snake," she whispered unevenly, enfolding him in her arms as he'd hoped she
would.

A few days later, Jillian smoothed her flowing off-the-
rack white lace dress; she gripped the seat of Cordell's
four-wheel-drive truck with her white elbow-length glove.
She stared at the Wyoming sunset. Cordell hadn't al-

lowed her time to change after their wedding in a small
chapel, and had insisted that his grandmother would love
to see his new bride in her "getup." The jet's steward-
esses had thought it was cute, the way the cowboy glowed
as he looked as his lace-dressed bride with her huge and
wilting daffodil bouquet. He handled her with so much
pride and gallantry that he frightened her badly. No one
had ever treated her as if she were delicate. Cordell insisted that she be comfortable and well fed. He had taken
off her heels and rubbed her feet, all the while looking at
her as if she were his special dessert and tonight was his
night to taste her. He'd made a mysterious reference to
getting her pink fuzzy slippers, as if they were something necessary to her. Jillian had clutched her bouquet
in fear, realizing that she was leaving everything that was
safe and worked for her.

Cordell was not an easy or safe man. He'd bristled
when she suggested they try a trial marriage. Or at least
go steady for a time. He didn't talk about his business,
and she sensed that he would play his man-provider role
and she would... *Would what?*

The hair on the back of her neck lifted. Why was she
in Wyoming, headed toward a ranch and Cordell's
Nanna Bear factory?

Why was this her wedding night? Why was Cordell
absolutely, primitively unshaven and grim-looking? Why
was he reluctant to answer questions about his grandmother's illness? Why did he look as if a dark, guilty secret lurked within him?

While Cordell concentrated on maneuvering around
holes on the road, she had time to focus on the past few
days. Cordell had apparently thought he was herding her
into a notion she might not like—that if he herded her

fast enough, she wouldn't have any choice but to marry him.

He was wrong. The whirlwind technique would not have made her marry him if she didn't want him. She'd watched him carefully and decided that she knew a good product when she saw one. Cordell never read the financial pages in the newspaper first; he read articles of human interest. He never passed a panhandler on the street without dropping money into the waiting cup, and he loved children and animals. Especially endearing to her was the way he stayed on one television channel, a genuine indicator that he was a long-haul man, for better or worse. There was a boyish, teasing side to him, like when he'd picked her up and run through the park's sprinklers.

Once, when they walked by a pawnshop, studying the contents in the dirty window, Cordell had said, "I wonder about the people who owned these things, the joy and the sorrow. What happened in their lives? Sometimes I buy a thing or two because there is a good feel to it, like someone loved it and it shouldn't go to those who don't care."

Atlas, who sorted out warm hearts from cold ones, hissing at people he didn't like, had leaped into Cordell's arms. Atlas had grinned and purred, draping himself, huge and hairy, upon Cordell's lap. Cordell hadn't been horrified by animal hair on his slacks.

Animals were not to be touched, according to Marsh. He had never once removed his suit jacket and tucked her in it, as Cordell had done when the wind turned chilly. Marsh would never, never gently lift her hair from under the collar. Cordell had listened very carefully when she explained about her family—that they worried about her and loved her. "You're their Miss Fix-It," he'd said flatly. "Don't worry, I'll take care of any fixing concerning you."

She wanted to do her share for him—an equal fixing.

Cordell wanted her desperately. Jillian had never experienced being the object of such heated, concentrated male desperation. When Cordell kissed her good-night at her apartment door, it had been with tenderness and longing, with heat lingering just a kiss away. He'd groaned achingly as he had moved her from him, striding quickly away.

Cordell had insisted on an old-fashioned wedding in the small chapel she had selected. Cordell had wanted her family to attend. She had resisted, unwilling to be criticized on her wedding day. Cordell had had a talk with her father, who scowled and turned red, and immediately clustered with her family. Stilted best wishes from her family had followed shortly. At the wedding, they had been careful not to associate with Jillian's catsup-factory friends. Her family had been aghast at the assortment of homeless people stuffing food into their pockets.

Squirrels had done an impromptu rap song about a Wyoming big-hat dude who got a lady with a soft heart. He started a verse about "married and doing it" just before Cordell grabbed his jacket and lifted him off the floor. Cordell had grimly whispered in Squirrels's ear and slowly lowered him. The boy instantly started a rap song about sweet brides, spring and daffodils.

Jillian had hurled her arms around her family, and for once they had returned her embrace. Buffy had patted a tear away from her eye. "What will we do without you, dear? You always make everything so right."

"That's your job now, Buffy," Jillian had stated gently. "You'll be fine, and I'll be back—" Then she'd realized that Cordell wanted the happy-couple playacting to continue for a short time. "We'll be back," she had finished.

"Don't call," Cordell had added in an ominous tone. "We'll call you." When she elbowed him in the ribs, he had grunted and showed his teeth in a tight rottweiler smile.

"Buffy, you'll be just fine," Jillian had said soothingly, noting the distress in her mother's expression. "You'll get the hang of it in no time."

Buffy's eyes lit with the new challenge. "Oh, dear, do you think I can manage without you?"

"Perfectly," Jillian had returned, very conscious of the glow inside her. The glow was a little like loving. She had suspected that she was falling in love with Cordell.

Her family had been oddly quiet as she and Cordell left immediately afterward for the airport. They loved her in their way, and she would miss helping them. Who would listen to them and help smooth out the crises? In the cab, she had cried on Cordell's shoulder and let him rock her. He'd drawn her upon his lap and cuddled her while she sobbed her heart out. The cabbie had kept looking back in his mirror, certain that Cordell had beaten her, even though it was the groom who wore the blackened eyes.

Cordell's truck hit a bump, dislodging her from the past few days. She glanced at him now—her brand-new husband—and repeated that she had wanted Cordell and she had wed him for herself. She'd already been through an unloving marriage, and his note caper—"promise to marry ASAP"—hadn't frightened her into anything. She wanted to claim him instantly. She'd taken an instinctive gamble on Cordell. As soon as she helped him through the passing of his grandmother, Jillian had decided, she would try to make their relationship as husband and wife work. All the indications were that they were sensually attracted and that Cordell's basic traits were exactly what she wanted. He fit her—it was just a matter of trimming off the rough edges, making him aware of a woman's delicate side, and tuning him into his feminine instincts. Relating skills took time to develop, and they would have a lifetime.

The truck hit another bump, and she glanced at her new husband, his jaw darkened with stubble. She hoped he was environmentally conscious and observed the cautious use of water. She'd heard that couples showered with each other to save water, and she wondered if Cordell would fit into the shower stall. She looked down his tall, powerful body and decided that he would fit just fine.

Cordell had ripped off his tie and dress jacket the moment they boarded the jet. He'd rolled up his shirtsleeves and opened his collar; he'd looked at her in the seat next to him and tenderly adjusted her seat belt. Though he had kept his distance throughout the past few days, staying at a motel, he was considerate. Cordell treaded very lightly, avoiding any possible argument. He wanted her to wear his mother's ring, though. No other woman had worn it, and the fit was perfect. His dark eyes held a satisfied gleam.

Jillian gazed at the sunset without seeing it. Cordell—her new groom—had two shiners, two beauts, two black and bruised eyes, due to her. She shivered, noting the soaring mountains of Wyoming, the lofty pine trees on the rough road to Cordell's ranch. Jillian sighed, overwhelmed by her current situation. "I'm not promising anything," she muttered, her uncertainties tugging at her. "This entire process was all too fast. I'm a person who likes to weigh alternatives."

There weren't any alternatives. She wanted Cordell desperately.

They hadn't had time to talk about each other's expectations. Or rather, Cordell was not a talker, she'd discovered in the past few days. He was a doer, and he kept his emotions locked inside.

She wanted a friend and intimacy.

"You're not promising anything. So you've said about a hundred times," he returned easily, slowing the truck. "Look." He nodded toward a small herd of deer grazing in a lush meadow.

"Ohhh..." she murmured appreciatively, inhaling the clean, fresh, pine-scented air. She allowed Cordell to slide his fingers through hers, the fit perfect and reassuring. She loved to cradle his little finger within hers.

"You're prettier than those deer," he said, as if testing the words. She realized that compliments were new to Cordell. She knew he'd been trying since she'd lectured him about not being romantic. "I didn't know you were a Horton, Jillian. That isn't why I wanted to marry you. I wanted you for you. Because..." Here, Cordell clearly floundered; he stared out into the Wyoming sunset. Because of her, he was trying to relate. He was trying to hug more, she noted, and remembered being slightly crushed after the small wedding. Cordell had lifted her in his arms and carried her down the steps, and had tucked her into the taxi before she could catch her breath.

Now here she was, about to meet his dying grandmother and present her with Cordell's two bruised eyes. "I'm sorry," she said again, looking up at him in the twilight. She touched his cheek lightly.

"How sorry?" he asked, in his intense, quick way, shocking her. She wondered if he had inherited his trapping instincts from his mountain-man ancestors.

"You know that was totally out of character for me—but you made me . . . you make me . . ."

He leaned closer. "Get this—I'm not making you. I am going to be romantic. Got it?"

His kiss began as a slow search for every contour of her lips, a nibbling on her lower one. Jillian tried to force her mind back to the lecture she'd intended to give him. "You . . . have to . . . learn . . . to relate more . . . to open up . . ."

"I'm trying," he whispered into her ear. "About opening up. Do you think you could open your lips for me? Or are you afraid of me? Let me in, dear heart. . . ."

"You're . . . kissing me," she reminded him, aware of the heat rising between them.

"Oh, hell. I hope I am. Either that or I'm dreaming. I haven't slept since meeting you," he murmured against her skin, his lips grazing her chin and nuzzling her jawline.

"Why not?" she asked, trying to force air into her lungs as Cordell continued kissing a trail to her locket.

"Do you always wear this?" he asked, tugging on the locket with his lips.

"Always." She gripped the front of his shirt, needing an anchor in an unsteady tropic storm.

Cordell's large hands were very gentle upon her breasts, gently caressing, so gently that she didn't notice his touch until it grew firmer, more seductive. He was treasuring her, she realized, learning the soft shape and weight with a reverence that caused tears to come to her eyes. In their few days together, he had been too respectful, and now she sensed that he was intent upon claiming her. . . .

She wanted with all her heart to touch his smooth, hairless shoulders. To grip them, and smooth them for a lifetime of resting her head upon . . . She glanced down to where Cordell had opened her lacy dress, to the lace of her peach bra. It looked incredibly fragile as Cordell's dark fingers smoothed her breast. "It's getting dark...." she managed as he bent to kiss the tip of her breast. "Ah...ah...shouldn't we be going?"

She reached to push his head away, frightened by the emotions leaping to life within her. At times she had glimpsed passion with Marsh, but Cordell caused her to want to forget her inhibitions and step into the fire.

His lips were hot now, moistening the lace over her nipple, enclosing the tender peak.

She realized she had torn his shirt open, popping the buttons, when his fingers tore her lace—and his mouth had found her softness, nibbling, kissing, heating her. And then, finally, there was the dark, elemental tugging of his mouth on her breast.

She had waited for this, she realized distantly...waited for Cordell. His hand was sliding up her thigh now, and he eased her beneath him.

He fit.

His weight pressed her gently into the pickup's bench seat, his heat and strength enfolding her and calming the desperate restlessness within her. "Cordell?" she asked, worried now, because everything was so right and yet she barely knew him. She'd dated, kissed, other men, and longed for a fit like this, the secure and lasting kind. She struggled to remember that she had married him to make his grandmother's last days comfortable.

His chest lowered to her breasts. Cordell eased his large hand around the nape of her neck, lifting her for a long, searching kiss that matched her lips perfectly. She tasted his tongue and locked her arms around him. His rapid heartbeat matched hers, and his heat penetrated her clothing. Again his hand found her thigh, skimming it lightly beneath the layers of lace and slip to press against her intimately. "Cordell?"

He groaned, trembling and hot as he lay upon her, his hardened body pressing down, seeking. Jillian trapped him with her arms and legs, lifting her hips to him, wanting him. Wanting to lock their lives and their bodies together. Cordell groaned deeply, shakily, and the tip of his tongue, tracing her ear, sent a frantic jolt throughout Jillian's overheated body. "I like kids," he whispered, his large hands stroking her gently. "Do you?"

"Yes," she managed as he opened his door and settled himself carefully between her thighs. Their legs dangled outside the pickup.

"Oh, God . . ." Cordell's deep voice was ragged as he found her garter snaps. He locked his fingers around them as if he had just discovered gold. "No panty hose. I thought all women crammed themselves into those things. Like sausages."

"I might have some in my trousseau," she offered, hoping that she hadn't disappointed him. Right now, she couldn't bear to have him leave her. Nothing mattered but The Fit.

Cordell went very still. "Your trousseau? Like sexy nighties?"

She blushed, and Cordell rocked her gently. "I can't very well sleep in the nude, you know, Cordell," she stated primly.

"We'll talk about that later, dear heart," he said huskily. She decided he was getting better about saying the right things.

Jillian could not resist running her fingertips over his shoulders. Cordell held very still. Then he levered himself up slightly, and when he settled once again upon her, Jillian realized that only her lace briefs separated them.

Cordell's trembling, reverent hands framed her hot cheeks. Then he kissed her, long and sweet, and she began to melt and quiver, and dug her fingertips into his shoulders.

"Jillian, I swear I do not want you because of your family's business. Do you believe me?" he asked earnestly.

She couldn't help arching against him. Above her in the moonlight, Cordell's features were harsh, and yet his expression was tender. "Do you, Mrs. Dougald?"

She kissed him for her answer, telling him how much she needed him. The urge rose up in her sharply, frantically. "Oh, honey," Cordell whispered unevenly as he kissed her breasts, suckling them and sending white-hot need ripping through her. "We'll do this better when we're in bed, I promise. Stop me now, if you don't want..."

She held his head to her, needing his hunger, needing his mouth upon her, needing the fit desperately.

Cordell's soothing fingertips slid beneath her briefs, and then he eased them away, tossing them onto the dashboard. He ripped off his shirt and slid her dress's sleeves from her. Then he began to kiss her hungrily, and she returned the feverish kisses, grabbing his ears to hold him to her open mouth. She wanted to hold the fever riding him, to take him and make him warm and cherished and a part of her.

Cordell shook, his breathing as uneven and rapid as her own, and his hands slid under her hips, lifting her—

A horse nickered in the distance, and Cordell lifted his head at the second sharp rap on the pickup's hood. He cursed and snarled over his shoulder, "Get the hell out of here. I'm on my wedding night with my bride."

"Your butt shines in the moonlight, chigger," a woman's rough voice noted cheerfully. "Always had a little no-account butt, ever since you were a young'n. So you finally got another one, huh? Get yourself off her, boy, so's I can say howdy. Say, what are you doing parked down here on this old bad road, when there's a spiffy new paved one?"

"This is supposed to be an intimate experience, for the bride and the groom. I was hoping for some privacy," Cordell said between his teeth as Jillian tried frantically to pull up her dress.

"Stop flattening her, boy. Let the girl up, so I can see her," Nanna persisted. "You got these windows so steamed up, I can't see much of anything but a lot of fuzzy blond hair. She's a city woman, I suppose, with outlandish ideas. Probably useless, too."

"Git," Cordell ordered tightly.

"Don't you tell me to git, boy," the older woman returned easily, and chuckled.

"Cordell, do something," Jillian pleaded, aware that Cordell was shaking fiercely. His scowl above her would have frightened a bear back into its cave. His steely body pressed intimately upon her.

"I'm going to wring her scrawny neck," he muttered, taking a fierce look down at Jillian. "She won't give up until she gets what she wants—a look at you," he added in a doomed, grim tone.

"Who is she?" Jillian tried a weak smile up at the round face peering down at her through the steamed windows. The brilliant flashlight beam hit her eyes.

"Nanna," Cordell said, his heart pounding against her palm. "I don't suppose you'd just mosey on out of here and let me and my woman have at it, would you?" he asked louder, in an angry tone that vibrated through the fresh spring air.

"Why, Cordell, honey," Nanna's rough voice returned in a sugary tone, "I never saw you so worked up over a woman before."

"She's not a woman. She's my wife." Cordell lifted slightly, groaned, and eased Jillian's lace skirt lower. His fingers pressed gently against her damp warmth, and he groaned louder, longingly.

He looked so shaken, hot and frustrated that Jillian almost smiled. Then a distant thought dropped into her reality. "Nanna? As in your dying grandmother? What's she doing out here?"

"Checking on this truck. Could be rustlers, you know. I haven't marked all the herd," Nanna stated cheerfully. "So old Cordell finally roped him another one," she mused as she drew out a pipe and lit it. "What's your name, honey?"

"Mrs. Dougald!" Cordell snapped. He had eased out of the pickup, and Jillian sat upright. He looked as though he wanted to murder the woman, who had just agilely swung up onto a huge horse. The horse reared in the moonlight, and Nanna waved her hat like Roy Rogers before slapping the flanks of the horse. Horse and woman raced off into the night.

Cordell slid into the pickup's cab. He gripped the steering wheel with both hands, glared at Jillian and demanded, "What?"

When she could talk, Jillian tried to keep her voice even. She wanted to scream. "So Nanna lives. You were just about to... You know what you were just about to do...."

"Hell, yes, I purely do," he snapped, raking his hands through his hair. "I was primed. You were, too."

"What? Primed? As in tuning an engine? And your grandmother is alive?" She fired the questions at him indignantly, shaking with anger. The emotion was new to her, brought to life by one Cordell Dougald, her new husband.

He raked his hands through his rumpled hair, making it stand out in peaks, and then ran his hand across his face. The sound of his beard scraping against his palm caused Jillian to sit upright and a long distance away from Cordell. "Nanna lives," she repeated ominously, glaring at him.

4

— ◄ —

"So. You roped yourself a city woman by using your poor old dying granny as bait, huh? Well, chigger, from the look on her face, you've got yourself one hot tamale," Nanna said in her rough, brassy tone. Nanna was ageless, dressed as always in worn, dirty denims and a flannel shirt. Her short gray hair was flattened by her western hat, and her aged leather boots were dusty. "You're hot for her, huh? I wondered when some little girl would knock you off your high horse. So what did you put in the prenuptial agreement this time, boy?" Nanna asked in Cordell's bedroom.

From what Jillian could see before Cordell had grimly carried her into the house, the sprawling home was western-style, with a huge front porch. Cordell had carried her across a spacious and sparsely furnished living room with a blazing fireplace and dumped her on a massive bed built of smoothly polished logs. He had slammed the door in Nanna's face, but she had entered with a broad grin. "Oh, these mountain men. It's bred into them, the bringing home of their wives and dumping them in that old bed."

Cordell didn't budge, glowering down at her, dark red color in his tanned cheeks. "They know what they want when they see it. His daddy was that way, and his daddy before him," Nanna continued, while Cordell and Jillian glared at each other and Jillian scooted off the bed.

"Come on out to the kitchen when you're ready," Nanna invited. "You may as well eat and get your energy up."

Cordell shot her a glare that could have started a forest fire. "I'm starting on your cabin out back tomorrow at first light."

"What prenuptial agreement?" Jillian asked when she could speak.

Cordell was looking at her tenderly, his dark eyes flowing over her tumbled hair, her kiss-swollen lips, and down to her bosom. Her breasts ached from his lovemaking, unbound and swelling as he stared at them hungrily.

She crossed her arms protectively. Mr. Cordell Dougald had lessons to learn. She spotted a bit of peach lace peeping from his pocket and jerked her panties from it. She stepped into them, arming herself to tear Cordell apart. She needed that fragile barrier desperately.

"You mean he didn't cover his bases and assets, making you sign a prenuptial agreement? Well, well!" his grandmother exclaimed curiously. "So old Cordell just reached and took for once, huh?"

"And I didn't marry you because of your family connections," Cordell said darkly before he reached for a battered western hat and other clothing hanging from a hook on the door. He jammed the hat on his head, pulled Jillian into his arms and kissed her with the heat that had blazed between them in the truck. "That's why," he muttered before he stalked out of the room.

Jillian realized in horror that tears were dripping from her eyes and that her heart was breaking. Nanna's strong arm went around her as she whispered gently, "Oh, that

Cordell. He's a doer, all right. Reckon he's got a thing or two to learn about wedding nights and brides. I'll bet he's kept his distance in an old-fashioned way, and now he's ready...well, he's ready.''

Nanna enclosed Jillian in her arms and rocked her. Jillian, who hadn't had harbors in her lifetime, clung desperately to Nanna. "Did you give him those shiners, little girl?"

Jillian sniffed and wiped her tears on Nanna's shoulder. She nodded, still appalled that she had used violence for the first time in her life. "So it's like that, is it?" Nanna murmured wisely.

"He's just awful. He tricked me into signing a statement that I would marry him, and then he said that his dying grandmother wanted to see him married before she died. That's not true, is it, Nanna?"

"Good Lordy, no. My mother lived to be over a hundred. I got thirty more years to go before they plant me. Cordell just wanted you, little girl. He's used to contracts and business, and can't quite make the grade where modern women are concerned. That's why he decided to marry those bloodless bony-butts, I reckon. They didn't ask much of him. He knows he's in trouble with you, and can't help himself. You're opening the door to his feelings, and he's kept that locked for years. I imagine old Cordell is pretty scared right now."

"It's our wedding night. I thought we would talk about our future and relate and..." Jillian wailed, wanting Cordell to hold her and cuddle her and—

"Shush. What's your name, anyway, little girl?" When Jillian told her, Nanna asked softly, "What does Cordell call you?"

Jillian rummaged through her limited stash of Cordell memories. "He'd just called me 'dear heart' before you arrived."

Nanna snorted. "He's old-fashioned, and that's what his daddy called his mama. So you're special. He'll come around. So now that you've discovered what a maverick he is, you'll probably just pack up and git, huh?" she asked softly, easing back to study Jillian.

The word *coward* lurked in Nanna's tone. And just a wisp of hope and longing. "He's awful," Jillian muttered, standing away from the older woman. "Just awful. 'Have at it.' What a way to describe making love. *It's our wedding night!*" she wailed again.

She stared at the foot she had just stamped, as though it didn't belong to her. All of this was Cordell's fault. He had to pay.

Nanna's strong arms encircled Jillian. "He's run off on that big black stallion, Nightmare. He'll lick his wounds, take a cold swim or two up at the camp, and come back after you've gone. Cordell doesn't like people to see him in his torment. He hid his grief after his folks and sister died in that plane wreck, and sometimes when that chigger goes riding off like all hell is after him, I know he's grieving still. Yep, old Cordell's out there, all alone on his wedding night, primed and hungry and hurting. He won't talk about it, just let himself fester and stew and terrorize the workers at Nanna Bear."

Nanna hitched up her worn denims. "Then he'll come after you. I'd advise you not to make things easy on him when that happens. That chigger has always gotten what he wanted too easy. He's a good boy, but a hard ride. Not an easy goer."

Jillian stepped back from Nanna and wiped her eyes. "He married me today, and he's just run off. Now that makes me mad, no matter what he did before. And, by the way, I'm not the running kind."

"Old Cordell is a believer in contracts, little girl. He won't be sharing himself with no other woman, not now that he's said his vows. Just how mad are you?" Nanna asked.

"Mad enough to go tell him off," Jillian retorted, furious now. Every nerve in her body was fired with the primitive frustration and anger that only Cordell could ignite. "Point me to his camp and give me something to ride."

"Eeyah!" Nanna yelled, and did a little jig on the board floor. "Now that's what I call action!"

The familiar mountain air enfolded Cordell. He walked the stallion to cool him in the night air, which was scented with pines and spring. Then Cordell tore off his clothes and plunged into the freezing waters of the small lake created by the melting snow. He'd hoped to gently claim his bride. He'd wanted to tell her with his body how much he cared before telling her about Nanna. Once Jillian had let him love her the way he wanted, she'd realize how she needed him. She was right for him, and talk just cluttered the air between them.

Jillian made his heart leap each time he looked at her.

Cordell launched himself out of the freezing water and wiped himself dry before sliding into his down sleeping bag. He studied the stars and tried to force away how much he wanted the woman who was now his—until she packed up and left in the morning.

He touched his bruised eyes lightly, reassuring himself of Jillian's passion. Then there was the humming tightness in his body that told him she had responded perfectly to him. She'd fly back to New York, to her Cling-ons, and maybe... Cordell gritted his teeth, realizing that he'd probably follow after a time, when he had a plan.

Tucked in his wildest dreams was the hope that Jillian would come after him, all sweet and shy and cute and hungry as she had been. He listened to the revving of Nanna's all-terrain vehicle coming closer, and shook his head. All he needed now was his grandmother's sage advice on handling women. He groaned in frustration, remembering how adorable Jillian had been in the small chapel this morning. How he wanted to make everything right for her, even with the cold Horton family. She loved them. She loved Atlas. Jillian was a soft, caring woman. He'd wanted her from the first moment he saw her. All cute and snuggly and warm, her fingers fitting perfectly with his...

Cordell sighed and braced his arms behind his head. He really loved how Jillian's smaller, softer hand fit his. A man could easily get used to a lifetime of that tenderness. That cute little mole beside her mouth was like a tasty little chocolate drop, the frosting on the heat and welcome of her lips.

Cordell thought about Jillian's eyes, as green and soft as the mountain meadows. He frowned, annoyed by the sound of the approaching all-terrain vehicle zooming toward him on the old road. Nightmare nickered and pranced on his light tether. It was Cordell's wedding night, and he was listening to a dirt rider tear up the countryside. He should be listening to the frantic beating of Jillian's heart as they made love.

Dear heart... Cordell wondered why he should be remembering the tenderness in his father's voice now. The endearment had slid across his lips to Jillian; it suited her. Why was he remembering glimpses of his boyhood with his parents and his baby sister? He shoved them away, as he had done for years.

"Cordell!" After the revving motor died, Jillian's call stopped Cordell's heartbeat and his breath. "Cordell!" she called, not in a tender bride's come-hither tone, but rather in that of a woman on the warpath.

He lay very still, watching her white gown sweep through the shadowy pines. He had never seen anything prettier than when she walked down the aisle to him— "What? You can't just come up here and destroy a man's peace, you know!"

The moonlight lit her hair as she crossed the small meadow to him, her skirts lifted in her hands. He caught the flash of her legs, and air hissed from his lungs. The moonlight caught each bounce of her breasts as she trudged toward him. She looked like a goddess.

Jillian walked straight to his sleeping bag and placed her foot on his chest. "You can't run away from me, Cordell. I won't have it," she said, breathing hard. "We have to talk."

He really appreciated the sweetheart cut of her lacy gown, and the way the moonlight stroked her breasts. "You're mad as a wet hen," he said as Jillian pushed back her hair to glare at him.

She sat down on him, straddling him on the sleeping bag. She quickly zipped up the sleeping bag with an air of a huntress bagging her prey. She didn't notice that his arms were still folded behind his head.

"Don't think you're running off before we have this conversation, Cordell. Now just why did you run off before we could talk?"

His bride had come after him. Cordell wallowed in that thought, happy as a clam. "I don't like needing you," he stated reluctantly. "It's hard."

She threw out a hand in a gesture of frustration and hitched up her tangled skirt. He admired the moonlight glinting off her pretty knees as she squirmed upon him, getting more comfortable. "Well. Okay. That's a start. We're relating. Now why?"

His hands found her ankles and locked on to them. She didn't seem to notice the slight tether. "Relate to me, Cordell. This is supposed to be our wedding night..."

Jillian stopped suddenly and looked around. Her hands locked to the bag over his chest. He didn't mind the slight pain when his chest hair was caught in the material. Jillian held on to him as if she were riding a wild bronco. He guessed he felt a bit wild with her bottom and thighs pressed against him.

"Cordell? Where are we? What's that noise?"

"Coyotes."

Jillian shivered and surveyed the night around them. "It's really cold up here, isn't it?"

"Gets that way at night." She looked so cute in the moonlight, he thought tenderly. His sweet little bride.

I never saw anything prettier than your mama when we got married, boy. His father's deep voice hovered around him, and Cordell frowned, uncomfortable with this intrusion from the past. *Someday you'll meet someone and feel that same way, if you're lucky.*

"Oh. Of course it's cold, it's a higher altitude." Jillian wrapped her arms around herself. "I wish you wouldn't scowl like that. *I'm* the one with a problem. I didn't bring a coat. I was so angry with you that I didn't think about anything but wrapping my hands around your thick, arrogant neck."

"You could do that in this sleeping bag," he offered, certain that she wouldn't want to be close to him.

"You rat. There you are, warm and toasty, while I'm freezing."

"Come into my parlor," he invited, wanting to cuddle her very close and make her truly his own, a part of him forever.

The right woman changes a man's thinking.... He starts thinking about forever and being a part of her and her of him. Cordell shook his head, shoving the past away from his wedding night. He hadn't let himself think of his parents since he was a boy.

"You can't be trusted," she whispered huskily. "You just dumped me on the bed. You started an argument with your poor dear grandmother, and then you ran away." Jillian dashed tears from her eyes. "I thought you might care, and I worried that you would break your neck before I had the chance."

"Stay with me, dear heart?" he heard himself ask unsteadily. He'd made her cry. A fist of ice slammed into him. He'd made her sad on their first day of marriage. Any minute, she'd run— "I need you," he heard himself say.

The statement was torn from his heart, reminding him briefly of how a little boy had cried for those he loved, who had deserted him. Cordell pushed the memory away and waited for Jillian to run. The need to have someone of his own squeezed his hammering heart.

He realized how lonely he'd been, how empty, before meeting her. Long ago, that little boy had promised not to open his heart again, and now Cordell's adult mind and body told him that he was not complete without this special woman.

He smoothed his thumb across her lips and drew a teardrop to his tongue, tasting it. No one had ever cried for him. He hadn't expected or wanted anyone to be close to him. But here Jillian sat, straddling him, uncertain, and he needed her.

She looked at him warily and dashed away another tear. "You probably say that to all your replacement women—that you need them."

"Not a one," Cordell replied honestly as he wiped his thumb lightly across one set of eyelashes, then the other. They felt like soft, damp fluttery feathers against his callused skin.

"What are you wearing under there?" she asked after a moment.

"Skin." He chose not to mention that his skin covered a hot, hardened body, aching for her. His fingertip circled her ear, investigating it, and she shivered.

"Oh." She eyed him carefully, then traced the bruised area around his eyes. Cordell liked her fingertip-play as she continued, "I really am sorry. Er... what did you mean when you told your grandmother that we were, ah... having at it? Exactly what does that mean? And did you bring that warehouse of prevention with you? Cordell, I don't think any human male could use that many in one year."

Cordell knew that the way he felt, he could come close to using the entire amount. But he didn't want to; he wanted to feel Jillian's moist softness, wanted to feel her take him completely and to free his urge to bury his life force deep within her welcoming, nurturing nest. After a lifetime with ranch animals, Cordell recognized the primitive need within him to release himself into the woman who fit him perfectly. "I didn't plan to use them at all," he tried softly, gripping her ankles tighter, in case he had messed up again. "I thought I'd ask you."

She held very still, bending slightly over him. "Why not use them, Cordell?"

"Has to do with the nature of man, and what he wants to leave behind," he advanced cautiously. He'd been thinking how cute she'd look, fluffy and round and soft, with his baby nestling inside her.

"Now that is deep thinking," she murmured, bending closer to lay her head upon his shoulder. "Tell me more."

Cordell swallowed, realizing that his ultimate test was expressing himself at the moment. He wrapped his arms around her and smoothed her back, loving how she nestled upon him. "Has to do with how I feel about you. I want you like I've never wanted another woman, dear heart. I want to be inside you, and I want it to mean something to you, too."

"Why, Cordell," she murmured, stroking his shoulders, "that is sweet."

"I've got a feeling for you, and it scares me," he added, encouraged.

Jillian lay very still upon him, and he rocked her in his arms. "Come be my wife, dear heart," he whispered against her ear. "Let me warm you with the fire burning in me."

"I guess I could do that," Jillian whispered unevenly after a while. "If it really means something to you. Does it, Cordell? I have to know that, for tonight, I am what you want."

"Oh, hell, yes!" The truth shot from him like a bullet into the night air. His hands trembled as he reached up to frame her jaw and slowly draw her mouth down to his. He tried to be patient, trembling, attempting to still his desire for her and to show her the gentleness he felt for her in his heart.

After a time, Jillian sighed. He watched, entranced, as she slid her dress over her head and tossed away her ruined bra. Cordell helped her into his sleeping bag and placed his arm around her; her head rested on his shoulder, and she lay beside him, his perfect fit. "You've got some good points, Cordell."

He nuzzled her hair, inhaling the flowery fragrance and bathing himself in his happiness.

She touched him accidentally; he held his breath as her fingers drifted back across his stomach, and then lower. Cordell reacted instinctively and eased over her, settling between her thighs, just as he had in the truck. "There's a feeling in me," he said, wanting her to know that this time was special to him, one that he would lock in his heart.

"You don't think this will last, do you?" she asked, sliding her arms around him.

"No. But you fill an ache in me that will last when it ends," he returned truthfully.

"I can handle that for now." Jillian moved gently, lifting her hips to him, and his mouth found hers. "We fit," she whispered against his cheek.

"Yes." Cordell smoothed her body, tearing away her briefs, and found her breasts with his mouth. He wanted to treasure her, to let her know how dear she was to him....

When he entered her and her cry flew across the night sky, Cordell knew that he had come home.

After the third time they made love, Jillian wilted upon his chest, muttering, "This is absolutely shocking. People don't make love like this."

Cordell grinned and stroked her hair, enjoying the warmth and softness of her body wrapped in his. He rubbed his chest against her breasts and began mentally designing a nightgown for his wife. One with sweet eyelet lace and accessible buttons down the front. A little gather and tucking at the bodice, allowing for the baby.

After he dodged the uncomfortable jab of her knee between his thighs, contentment washed over him. She was his now. He'd claimed her, and she'd given him everything, in little sighs and kisses and meeting him at the ultimate moment with an expression he'd never forget. He dozed lightly, aware that he wanted her again. He didn't mind the small jabs of her elbow into his ribs at all. Jillian nestled closer, and Cordell smoothed her warm, pliant body against him. She was the perfect fit, and he adored her. He kissed the top of her head and gathered her closer. Everything would be just fine, now that she was his.

Jillian awoke at sunrise. Her stomach was grumbling, and Cordell was filling her again. She flung herself into the fire, and their lovemaking was as hungry as the first time. Later, she lay nestled in his arms, her bridal status complete, the man she cared for deeply pleased with her. She knew instinctively that he was happy; the lines around his mouth had eased, and his warm and tousled, boyish look was endearing. His look down at her body, tangled with his, was tender, yet fierce.

"Well, that's that," Cordell said in a supremely pleased voice. His tone rang with the finality of a man scoring a baseball home run.

"Hmm? What did you say?" Jillian smiled drowsily, remembering how her mother had instructed her to stick pins in Cordell's prevention. She wanted his children, and welcomed the dream that they might have created a new life between them.

Cordell yawned and stretched beside her. "I said, that's that. We're married, dear heart."

She smoothed his chest, aware of how her body tingled and ached from his lovemaking. How all of her little intimate muscles had clung to him... But there would be more to their happiness, the blending of their lives, each meeting the other on equal ground, creating a relationship that would last when they were aged and rocking by the fire. Or rocking babies to sleep... "Yes. I think a rocker would be nice in the living room."

"Whatever you want to do in the house is fine. You're mine now," he whispered against her hair.

"Yes." She hugged him, her tender lover, her groom of one day, with a lifetime ahead of them. "And you're mine."

He lay too still against her. "You're mine, aren't you, Cordell?" she asked, needing his reassurance. "As in an equal partnership?"

The sunrise stroked pink over the rugged Wyoming mountains and their sleeping bag. "I've never thought of it like that," he said after a time.

His bride lay very still. "It's a half-and-half deal, Cordell, lover, sweetheart," she stated carefully, and frowned when he didn't answer. She flung out a hand and latched on to his chest hair, tugging it. "Isn't it? Or am I just the little wife replacement? The vacancy filler? Cordell, did you mean what you said about needing me? Or are you on the rebound, and this is a pride thing?" She flushed and realized that a man like her new husband definitely needed a woman.

"I need a wife," he said, easing her hand away from his chest. "I'll take care of you, and you can do for me. I'll give you a household checkbook when we get back. I'll get you those pink fluffy house slippers wives wear."

"*Do?* What does that mean, *do?* What do you mean, *take care of me?* As in, the little woman stays at home while the caveman goes out and earns a living?"

"Well, uh...something like that," Cordell admitted as she disentangled herself and scrambled out of the bag. She dressed furiously and shoved away Cordell as he came to hug her from the back. She turned to him, shaken by the sight of Cordell's naked body standing in the sunrise, all glorious corded muscle and arousal. She looked up at his face, noted the bruises around his eyes, and said very carefully, "Now get this. I am a person with needs to accomplish things. To develop and use my skills. While you are making me a part of your life, consider that you are also a part of mine. You didn't claim me, Cordell Dougald. *I* claimed you. *I* married you because *I* wanted you. *I* reached out and *I* took you. Got it?"

Cordell snorted in disbelief and placed his hands on his lean hips. "That's not the way it works."

Jillian ignored the sharp tug of desire, her body freshly awakened by his. "You are wonderful and sweet. But sometimes you are so narrow-minded that I could wring your neck. I want our relationship to be balanced."

"Just tell me if you intend to use one of those...those female appliances while we're married," he demanded, looking at her darkly. She refused to fall for his rumpled, sexy male look. "And then let's not talk about it again."

"It is every woman's right to explore her sensuality," she returned evenly, pushing her mussed hair behind her ear and refusing to be forced into corners she hadn't explored.

"The hell it is," Cordell yelled indignantly, shattering the quiet mountain morning. "Not *my* wife."

"*Yours?* As in a refrigerator? Or a car? Or anything useful?" She thrust out her hands and sent him plunging into the cold water of the lake. Cordell surfaced with a roar of anger. She began running when he launched himself onto a grassy ledge. He looked like a mountain man out to stake his claim.

At ten o'clock that morning, Cordell realized that his bride's back was stiff and unwelcoming. He wondered if he could sneak up on her and slide his arms around her waist and nuzzle her cheek before she hit him again. Her bridal dress was slung over a rack of chambray blouses with crocheted lace insets, and she was wearing one of them, with a matching long skirt. The Native American moccasins on her feet—probably a gift from Jessica Blueheart—were silent as she tapped her toe and flipped through the records in his factory office and studio.

Cordell shivered mentally. His bride had invaded his creative nest, where no one else dared to tread. She braced her hip against his drawing board and readjusted his overhead lamp. Jillian glanced at him, and he froze in the doorway. "Are you going back to New York?" leaped out of him in the next heartbeat.

"Should I?" she asked coolly, looking at him over her glasses.

"I'd just follow you when you cooled off," he said truthfully, aching to hold her. Fear rode him; he realized that the last time he felt that emotion as deeply had been when his parents' plane was discovered missing.

"Well. Then we'll just have to settle everything right here, won't we?" she said. "Oh, by the way. I've just discovered that not only do you own Nanna Bear, *you're* the Nanna Bear designer. How nice. My new husband didn't tell me that important detail of his life...that he's a tip-top designer. You're *very* talented."

"It's not important." He'd let few people in on his secret—only those who needed to know. Sharing himself with anyone wasn't easy. He wanted Jillian close to him now, without the pressure of telling her his secrets. They were rusty and old and covered with hours of brooding and pain; Jillian represented a fresh start, a joyous discovery that there was happiness waiting for him. "We could take a horse ride, look at some old mines," he offered uneasily as she flipped through his sketchbook of new designs. He wanted to show her where he'd grown up, and maybe lay her down in the soft meadow grass.... He decided to offer her a womanly entertainment. "Or we could go down to the house and you could maybe, ah...order some furniture or rugs and kitchen things."

She looked up at him coolly, and he floundered. Jillian smiled tightly. "So you'd prefer me in my little-nestmaker role. Right, Cordell? You really don't want to share your life with me, do you? You have your role, and I have mine?"

"You talk a lot," he stated, realizing that a flush was rising up the back of his neck. "There's nothing wrong with a man wanting to make a living—"

"Bring home the bacon?" she supplied too softly. Her round glasses glinted in the sunlight passing into the room from the large studio windows. "And my role is to cook it, I suppose?"

"The workmen have arrived to build Nanna's house. You could help her lay out the design." He'd offered a woman thing to do, the pleasure of making nest and home. Something to entertain her and to fill her hours without him.

Jillian's hand smoothed his sketchbook, the one that no one else dared touch. "But." The word was like a shotgun blast into his uneasy nerves. "But, Cordell, I have other plans."

That sentence made the hair on the nape of his neck stand up. From the corner of his eye, he saw that the

Nanna Bear workers were watching curiously. His head pattern maker and seamstress, Amanda Blackfeather, was grinning broadly. She'd always told him that "someday a girl will trip your trigger" and he'd fall like a brick wall. Pete Jackson, loaded with eyelet and chambray yardage, peered over it and winked.

Cordell closed his studio door. He didn't want the packing and shipping staff to know that he'd lost his groom-and-husband status after just one night. "What plans?" he asked warily.

Jillian looked around the spacious, well-lit studio. She fingered a swatch of chambray and another of intricate crocheted lace. "There's room for me in here, Cordell."

Slightly panicked, he looked around the room. He propped his boot on a chair, barring her way. He hoped he didn't look like an Alamo defender. "Not much. You'd be cramped. What do you want to do here?"

"It's called sharing lives and work," Jillian said softly. "Get used to it, Cordell."

He floundered a bit, feeling his kingdom slipping away from him. A fearsome insight loomed before him. "So this is it, right? The battlefield?"

"Something like that. I'd say it was more like sorting out the fundamentals we skipped before we were married. By the way, I do not like being tossed on the family bed like your latest booty."

"I work alone," he insisted, taking a step back as Jillian began moving a large table to one side. His stacks of fabric swatches tumbled, and his favorite scissors clattered to the littered floor. Jillian reached for a broom and began sweeping. "Don't...don't throw anything away...please," Cordell ordered when he could.

He reached out to grip her lace wedding dress as an anchor. Jillian had the ability to unnerve yet fascinate him. His biggest fear shot out of him. "Are you staying?"

"Can you cook?" she countered softly, sitting down to click on his computer. She flipped neatly through the programs and fastened on his bookkeeping—invoices and payments.

"What's that got to do with anything? Uh..don't erase anything, will you?"

Jillian turned slowly to him, her glasses glinting. "The catalog and computer shopping idea will work. We'll need a good photographer, and you'll need to take me through every procedure of Nanna Bear garment-making. I want to know Nanna Bear inside and out, and everything you have on that incredible lace."

Lace. Cordell glimpsed the twin mounds of her breasts rising into the sunlight. She wasn't wearing her bra. He'd have to give to get. He'd have to share or lose her. Jillian stood there, a determined woman meeting her challenges, head lifted, chin out, and every inch of her—

Cordell began to perspire. "You're not going to make this easy, are you?"

"I've only just begun," Jillian returned, with the air of a general on a mission. Then she turned back to the computer and began clicking away.

While Cordell was wondering if he could just slip over to her and soothe his troubled life with a kiss or two, Jillian turned to him. "You need a workers' day-care center, Cordell. If we're taking Nanna Bear Creations out of Wyoming and into the big world, we want to look good. I'll check into personnel records later, and the health care and retirement plans."

Cordell wondered who she was while Jillian turned to the computer and began feverishly clicking keys, ignoring him completely. He had just finished running his hands through his hair and across his face when she turned to him suddenly. She murmured sadly, "Cordell, take a note. Brides need kisses."

In a heartbeat, he was across the room and lifting her into his arms. She locked her arms around him and kissed him, matching his hungry urgency.

Cordell closed his eyes, nuzzled her cheek and smelled her hair. Everything was going to be just fine—setbacks were expected.

"We're sleeping separately tonight," she whispered against his throat as Cordell lowered her down onto a sturdy table.

He had just managed to get her skirt out of the way, to stand between her thighs and fill his hands with her breasts. "Sleeping together is a fundamental of married couples," he noted, wondering what ship he had missed. One heartbeat ago, she'd been sailing toward him again—

Jillian cuddled to him, laid her head upon his chest and held him and whispered, "But, honey bear, I can't think when you . . . you know . . . when you get amorous. All I can think of is getting the fit right, and . . ."

"Oh, hell, I'd like to." Yet the knowledge that he affected her pleased him, and he found himself looking deep into his wife's steamed glasses. He realized he was preening mentally about her "honey bear" endearment. It was like a little sweet hug.

"Are you going to give me that tour?" she asked huskily.

5

Cordell studied the bathroom one last time. Then he quickly lowered the toilet seat; he'd once heard a married woman with boys complain about men in the bathroom. Cordell did not want Jillian to hurt any part of herself because of him.

Jillian, his bride of two days, wouldn't leave the computer. Her fingers whizzed over the keys when he wanted them lingering over him. Cordell ripped a notepad from his jeans and slashed out a note to purchase equipment for a home office. He knew that women kept recipes, record collections, household inventories and genealogy records on computers.

With Nanna camping in her tent in the backyard, he'd have Jillian to himself on their second day of marriage. Separate bedrooms weren't on his menu of life. A trucker had delivered their packed boxes from New York. Cordell worried that Jillian might make herself at home alone in one bedroom—so he had hurried to place her clothing in the closet next to his, her bath powder and toothbrush near his. He thought her feminine little bottles looked sweet sitting next to his after-shave.

He rubbed his back. Scrubbing and waxing floors was . not fun. He frowned and noted the roughness on his hands, created by cleaning the two bathrooms, and quickly rubbed Jillian's hand cream into his skin. He lingered over the scent and thought how cute she was there in his studio, looking all curvy in his creations, with her baseball cap on backward, punching buttons. While she was visiting with Amanda, he'd taken a backup of his computer system, so that she wouldn't lose Nanna Bear's records.

He smelled the pot roast cooking in the kitchen, and quickly lifted the towel he'd been dusting with and fanned it, pushing the scents into the living room. He fluffed the pillows on his couch and frowned, standing back to survey his house. It was clean, but barren, offering little comfort. Except his hunting rifles, neatly oiled and in their rack. And his stuffed Canada goose, the champion set of deer antlers, and the trophy trout.

Cordell tilted his head to listen to Jillian rev the all-terrain vehicle's motor as she came down the hill from the plant. His bride, coming to him... Cordell kicked one of his socks beneath the sofa and ripped Nanna's huge apron from him. He balled it and stuffed it behind his gun rack. He glanced at the table, set for two, with candles ready. He hurried to light them and turn down the pot roast. The bakery cake and the wine were on the counter for after dinner. He'd never realized how much time it took to shop for and unload groceries.

Cordell tapped his fingers on the kitchen counter, surveying his handiwork, then glanced at the closed bedroom door. He swiftly opened it and turned down the bed's sheets—an invitation to slide into them. He puffed the pillows and artistically arranged the nightgown he'd made for Jillian. He'd placed a wrapped mint on the pillow, just as he'd seen done in hotels. He jerked down the shade, a preparation for an early bedtime and lingering lovemaking in the morning. Cordell stood very still, listening to the approaching vehicle, then quickly went around the entire house, lowering all the blinds to darken the house. He grabbed a fluffy quilt he'd just purchased and folded it beside the softly flickering fireplace. He'd always wanted to make love in front of the fire....

He rushed to the bedroom closet to retrieve his traveling shaving kit. He plucked out the strip of prevention and tore the packets into two separate lengths, tucking one part under the pillow without the candy. He placed the other part under the quilt. Jillian might have reconsidered the use of prevention.

An old memory flashed through him, locking his boots to the floor: how happy his father had been when Cordell's baby sister was born. A huge, silent man, his father had wiped away tears roughly and had clasped the tiny bundle to his heart; Cordell's tall father had cooed and glowed as he held his daughter.

Cordell pushed away the sudden, painful memory. There had been others looming around him since he'd married, troubling him. He hurried back to the kitchen to rip open the refrigerator door. The florist's red rose was there, and the orange juice for the bride's breakfast in bed.

He was panicked, he realized. Stunned by Jillian's inspection of Nanna Bear and her precise questions, he'd wanted to show her that he cared that she cared. He'd escaped to shop and clean and cook, to make everything appealing to her, including himself.

Missy Doors had been helpful in his desperation; she'd helped him select several pairs of silk boxer shorts. Though he preferred old-fashioned white cotton briefs, Missy had assured him that these were the big-city kind that men wore now. Wearing shorts that slithered on his behind and partway down his thighs was a small price to pay in his pursuit of a second wedding night. Cordell moved restlessly within his new silk shorts and tugged uncomfortably at his new jeans. They were stiff, and he refused to ask Nanna to wash them. He didn't want her in his operational vicinity tonight.

Cordell glanced at the old sewing machine and the scraps of the nightgown material around it. He jotted down a sketch for a new gown with a ruffled hem. The idea of Jillian wearing something he'd created especially for her and hadn't come off a store rack warmed him. The gown he'd just made was very simple, with larger buttonholes than were actually required. After one last searching look, Cordell went to meet his bride.

She'd scared him a little as he took her through the plant. Her expression had closed, as if she were concentrating on something within her. He hoped it was her need of him.

Jillian looked so cute, his little bride coming home to him. He recognized that she had needed time to console herself and do whatever women did before settling into a marriage. Dolf Green said that women had moods and snits and sometimes were best left alone to chew on their problems. Dolf said that, by and by, women came around if left alone. But he'd warned that if bothered, they'd dig in their heels, and no sweet talk could change their wet-hen moods. Cordell realized that he'd never considered women's moods, but it was important that Jillian was happy.

The night wind played in her hair, fluffing it around the ball cap she wore. With the wind tugging at her light chambray blouse and skirt, molding it to her, she looked perfect. His aching back, his frantic purchases and cooking, the new jeans and silk shorts and the extraclose shave were all worth the effort.

Jillian trudged up the front porch, carrying a briefcase, which she handed to him. She placed the ball cap in his free hand. She stood on tiptoe to give him a kiss that swished softly across his cheek before he could get real lip-to-lip contact. "Oh, hello, Cordell," she said tiredly, passing by him and into the house. "We're invited to Amanda's tomorrow night. It's a shower."

He closed the door to his lair after checking to see that Nanna was nowhere around. "A shower? That's for women, isn't it?" After a moment in which he watched her roll her shoulders, stretch and yawn, he added warily, "How many men will be there?"

"It's a wedding shower. I'm certain there will be some men there." Jillian placed her hands on her waist and stood looking at his stuffed goose, his trophy fish and his antlers. "What are these dead things doing on the wall?"

"How many? Who?" he demanded, alarmed at the idea of being surrounded by women without the protection of another male. As much as he wanted to show off his new bride, he wasn't going to a woman's party without a covey of men at his side. He smoothed the feathers of his beloved goose for comfort.

"Mmm...smells good," Jillian was saying, moving past him into the kitchen. "You know, Cordell, I was thinking that with all the work I did today, we might go shopping for household things tomorrow."

"You can buy whatever you want."

"Whatever *we* want. I wouldn't think of buying anything without you. We do need to move fast, because we're having a business party here in two weeks. That will be the the middle of May, the perfect time to launch out into marketing. Just in time for coverage for the June bride magazine issues. A little late, but I'll make calls so they can reserve space for us. We don't have time to waste. You'll need a spring and summer line worked up and ready to go. Sketches will do. The photographer says he'll start shooting products tomorrow. His work is good. Amanda is writing down the fabric content and cost of each garment. We're doing a special insert on the lace.''

"Photographer?" Cordell remembered asking Ace Darkwood if he could stop by with his camera. Ace took pictures for the local small-town newspaper, as well as wildlife shots that he sold to tourists as postcards.

"Those stuffed dead things on the wall frighten me." Jillian lifted the lid on the pot roast. She frowned and said, "Beef," in a condemning tone. She turned to him. "Cordell, I don't eat beef. Haven't you noticed?" she asked, in a small, hurt voice.

He realized belatedly that he'd been too busy staring at her lips as they opened and closed to notice her diet. "It's all I know how to cook," he said truthfully after a full moment. "We could go down to that pasta place in town."

But that meant sharing his woman with others on a night when he was primed for new-husband business. Cordell hoped she wouldn't accept his halfhearted offer. Because he wanted to show his goodwill, and because he knew that if she was offended by the stuffed trophies he probably wouldn't make love to her in front of the fire-place, Cordell snatched them from the wall and carried them out to a storage room.

"Pasta would be great, but I'm too tired to go out. If beef juices don't touch them, potatoes and corn are just fine. I appreciate your awareness of my sensitivity to dusty dead things," Jillian noted when he returned. "Cordell, come sit down. I want to show you some-thing."

When she picked up the briefcase, Cordell noted that the sofa seemed very small for making love. He grabbed the fluffy new quilt and opened it in front of the fire, nudging the protection under the quilt with his toe. He hoped she'd buy a big sofa, the kind that would suit lovemaking and cuddling in front of the fire.

"Why don't we sit on the floor? Would you like a glass of wine before dinner? Then we'll eat." She'd need energy to match the plans he had for tonight. He'd thought constantly about the three times they'd made love on the mountain, and he knew that he was up to breaking that record tonight. He quickly poured the wine, while she spread out papers on the quilt. As an afterthought, Cordell tossed the sofa pillows to the quilt and took out his pocket notepad. He glanced at the pillow, gleaned from a booth at the county fair. With faded gold lettering and fringes, it didn't seem like something he wanted to lay his bride's head upon. She watched him carefully as he scrawled *Soft pillows.*

He glanced down at her and added *Lots.* Jillian was frowning up at him. "Notes," he explained, easing onto the quilt with her.

The moccasins and socks were just the first of her clothing to be shed, he thought as he rubbed her feet and sat close to her. She met his testing kiss with a sweet, light one and sighed, leaning against him. "Thanks. I've heard husbands were good for this sort of thing after a hard day."

He beamed internally. He'd passed one test. He gently reached to unfasten her blouse's first button. "Just making you more comfortable, dear heart."

She placed her head upon his shoulder, and Cordell closed his eyes. "Ah...maybe we should take a nap before dinner? I'm a little tired, too."

"No, I'm excited about this project. I want you to see what I've done. Now, if you don't like it, we'll work on another angle. But I think that this is a good beginning."

He glanced at the roughly sketched layout sheets in her hand, the beginnings of a catalog. "The lace, Cordell. We'll do an inside story on the lace. On the women who crochet it, and a story on you, how you got the idea for Nanna Bear. Personal stories are appealing in catalogs. The women have agreed to act as models for an extra fee, and Ace is ready to get started tomorrow. Therefore, we're starting the day-care center at the factory tomorrow. Everything is working out so nicely, but we're really under pressure to make that deadline in two weeks for the launch of Nanna Bear." She continued to outline her ideas while Cordell studied her layouts.

"This is a catalog," Cordell said, turning the sketches slowly. "Who did this?"

"It's what I do, Cordell. What I did before quitting Horton's. What do you think? Before you say anything, just look at my marketing proposal. The first thing is to get the catalog out there, and then we'll start a computer ordering service. We'll have to revamp marketing—instead of only selling in bulk to stores, we'll get individual orders through an 800 number. The readjustment will boost profits by forty percent. A new line of accessories to go with the Nanna Bear lines would sell like hotcakes. Purses and belts with the Honey logo. Shoes... and I think a distinctive line of jewelry for women and little girls. A Nanna Bear line for little girls—matching mother-and-daughter designs—would send sales through the roof. Meanwhile, I think we should look at detergents and fabric softeners. Wash-and-wear clothing needs careful care. Why not create and market the very best?

We could test-market right here in Wyoming. By the way, I think Nanna Bear needs a full-time accounting department."

"I do that," he stated slowly, with the sands of his kingdom ebbing and flowing beneath his boots. "I've worked on accounts payable and receivable every Friday afternoon for the last ten years."

"And you did a good job, too, Cordell," she murmured soothingly as she patted his hand. "But a tip-top accounting department can provide marketing information and graphs at a snap of their fingers. A good corporate accountant can save a bundle on taxes, and is worth the paycheck. I know one of the best, who would like to work in the West. Harry is a love. He'd be here with bells on."

Cordell blinked down at his wife, who was watching him worriedly. She fit her hand to his while he reeled at the information that he had married a marketing expert. He had built his business from the start, sewing the easier designs while Amanda did the finish work. His one-man kingdom was endangered by the woman he wanted to care for, to provide for and to protect. She looked up at him, her green eyes dark with concern. "Cordell, you don't have to agree to any of this. It's just ideas. I want to help."

"Very expert ideas," he said slowly, instantly recognizing the professional layout. He sensed that his love-making plans for the evening had been swept away by a fast-moving whirlwind called Jillian. He reeled at this new aspect of his woman, whom he wanted to provide for and fix for, and who in return would make their nest perfect. He turned slowly to look at her, this new tip-top financial and marketing wizard-woman he had married. "Who are you?" he asked finally.

Jillian fought the terror seizing her, dragging her into a dark bog of memories. Cordell's expression was blank, as in "This does not compute."

"I am a marketing genius," she informed him sadly, weighted by her past. At an early age, her father had discovered her talent and had placed her in front of a computer when she should have been discovering boys. A hotshot wizard by the time she graduated from college, Jillian had dressed in business suits, flew around the world and pulled coups that seemed impossible. Once given a task, she'd been relentless, challenged down to her core. The competitive, sharpshooting young and hungry businesswoman who thought marketing and advertising were games. She was very tough, she had realized belatedly, uncaring for the personal traumas around her. Back then, she'd been a true profit-and-loss Horton, even if not in looks.

Jillian studied Cordell's face, seeing the lines there deepening in his confusion. The adorable space between his eyebrows narrowed. Nausea clawed at her, and she realized vaguely that she had been so excited that she hadn't eaten.

She'd decided at the instant she decided to marry Cordell—the instant when he did not pick up the television remote control and flip to another station during commercials—that she had to be truthful about who and what she was. This morning, while she was munching on a bean-filled burrito dipped in strawberry yogurt, she'd known that she could not begin their marriage in a disguise.

Her Horton blood was shameless when it came to marketing talent. She'd repressed it, but with the advent of Cordell into her life, her talent had leaped to life. She wanted everything, including her fulfillment as a talented businesswoman. She wanted the entire enchilada, a husband and a career outside of wifehood.

Her first marriage had failed because it was based on untruths. To soothe Marsh's unstable ego, she had denied some of her talents and had helped develop his. She'd become the perfect, supportive corporate wife, and because Marsh wanted to be the breadwinner in the family, she had pushed her skills into a box labeled The Wife.

The discovery that she liked people, really cared for them, had become during that time. She'd begun working for glossy professional charities and realized how much of what they took in did not go to the needy. She'd realized that a highly publicized project had cost the savings of elderly people who could not afford to give. Marsh had laughed and, after a heated argument, she'd learned that he'd had several affairs during their two-year marriage.

Deeply wounded, she had walked away and left everything, to devote herself to helping those she could.

Belatedly Jillian realized that she was speaking softly as she looked into the fire. She looked up at Cordell and found him staring at her as though she had sprouted another head. She'd married him while in disguise. She'd lose him now, but she was determined to be truthful with him and with herself. He looked so lost, so shaken, that burning tears began to form behind her lids. She felt old and weary. She would not fit into a housewife's fuzzy pink slippers.

"Did you love Marsh?" Cordell asked slowly, looking at her layouts, running his fingers over them, as if drawing the impressions into him, turning them over in his mind.

"I thought I did. He was an up-and-coming executive. The perfect match, or so said my family. At the time, I thought so, too. But I won't settle for hiding what I am again, Cordell.''

''I see. You are very good.'' His words were reluctant and admiring. She longed for an endearment at the end of them.

''Thank you.'' Jillian rose slowly and found her way into the bathroom. She shed her clothing and stepped into the shower, wishing the steaming water could wash away the fear that her second marriage was floundering. That after all she didn't fit the man who had made love to her beautifully. She had ached and glowed with the memory throughout the long, hard workday. He had touched her reverently, as if she'd break within his arms, beneath him. Until his passion had ridden him gloriously, and then he'd been hers, fierce and strong, and she'd let go of all restraints.

But it wouldn't be enough. She couldn't be his little nestmaker and still be true to herself. Eventually the bricks of a relationship based on untruths would begin to crumble. Cordell was now lodged deep within her heart; she couldn't hurt him, nor could she lie about herself, about how the challenge of marketing products excited her.

Her designs for the sample catalog were the best she'd ever done; it was as if her talent had been waiting to erupt at peak performance.

She dragged herself from the shower and padded to the closet, where she saw her clothes neatly hung beside Cordell's. She saw for the first time the bed and the tiny chocolate candy on the pillow. She glanced back into the bathroom and noted her toiletries neatly arranged beside his.

Nanna was very thorough. Jillian noted the nightgown on the bed; though it wasn't hers, clearly it was for her use. She drew it on and hovered over the sprawling king-size bed that did not contain her husband.

She was empty, drained by work and fear. She'd shared her deepest flaw with Cordell. Marsh had said that no man could tolerate a whiz like herself, especially if she was in his business arena. Cordell was an old-fashioned man, one who wanted to provide for his family. Jillian's shoulders slumped as she admitted that she'd lost again.

Cordell hovered uncertainly in the doorway. He carried a sandwich plate and a glass of milk. "You need to eat something. I made a peanut-butter-and-jelly sandwich."

"I'm scared," she blurted out, and couldn't prevent the tears from slipping down her cheeks.

Cordell took a step backward, fear in his expression. "Don't...cry. I don't know what to do when women cry."

She brushed away tears with her hands. "I'd really like this project, Cordell. It will be my best challenge yet. I need it, just like I need you. If you want, I can move out and—"

"Move out?" he roared indignantly after a moment. "But I've just got you!"

"Stop yelling. You're so emotional. *I've* just got *you*," she said lightly. "We can maintain a business relationship until the project is finished and Nanna Bear is out there in catalog form and on the shopping networks. I worked with Marsh after our divorce."

He glared at her. He walked to her, shoved the plate into one of her hands and the glass of milk into the other. Cordell framed her face with his hands and took her mouth hungrily. He smiled nastily when the hot, hard kiss was finished. "Now get this, dear heart. I am not

Marsh. I am in for the long haul, and I know the value of exclusive rights.''

His gaze ran hungrily down her, and the air stirred with tropic heat between them. ''I made that thing with extralarge buttonholes, for the nervous, ready-for-action new husband. Do you think it will sell?''

She gripped the sandwich plate and the cold milk as she looked down at the nightgown she wore. Soft and sweet, in light lace and chambray, the design was beautiful, drifting down to her toes. Except for the buttonholes. They were overly large. ''You did this?''

''Sewed it on my little sewing machine. The permanent design will have ruffles around the shoulders and the hem. I'm not good at ruffling, and I had to work fast. I don't have any experience at being the little nestmaker. I'd appreciate it if you wouldn't cry. You just bring home as much bacon as you want, darling.'' Cordell gently pushed the tip of his finger upward on her chin, closing her parted lips. Then he kissed her lightly, sweetly. ''*Darling.* I like that word. Suits you. What about starting a Darling line for those little girls you want to dress? I'd like to have a little girl, would you?''

Jillian sniffed. She knew that Cordell would agree to anything, say anything, to keep her from tears. He probably didn't mean what he said about bringing home the bacon. Clearly worried, he looked at her. She tried a wobbly smile and found herself yawning. Cordell stepped back, as if he feared the yawn was a prelude to another crying jag. ''Hold me,'' she said, placing the plate and milk glass aside to move into his arms.

Cordell folded her tightly against him, then swept her up into his arms and carried her to the fireplace. He lowered her to the quilt and lay holding her in front of the fire. She drifted off to sleep with the sound of his heart beneath her cheek. She was where she wanted to be.

The third day of their marriage, Cordell stared at Jillian as she tested the furniture store's rocker. An old-fashioned design, the huge rocker moved back and forth in the sunlight passing through the store's window. He heard his mother humming peacefully as she had rocked his baby sister, nursing her. Then, when the baby slept, his mother had drawn her upon his lap and rocked him, too. Love of the closest kind had enveloped him, and their hardships hadn't mattered. Pain slammed through him, and he looked away, not seeing the rest of the furniture.

"Cordell?" Jillian frowned lightly at him. Then she rose to draw him back to the chair. She sat upon his lap and stroked his frown away, and his momentary pain eased. Dismissing the beaming store clerk, Cordell gathered her close against him, rocking away in the display window. She gave him peace, and he sank into it. Why was he remembering his boyhood now? He'd fought to drag himself from poverty, remembering the hard times. Now, with Jillian in his arms, he was remembering love.

Moments later, he realized that a crowd with dreamy smiles had formed outside the window.

He quickly shifted Jillian from his lap and stood, scowling at the people watching them. Jillian's kiss on his cheek drew his attention back to her, and he said, "It's fine. We fit... Ah...we'll take it if she likes it."

"I do," she said, in the same firm tone she had used when taking her vows, her green eyes soft upon him. It was enough to make him want to buy the store's entire stock of furniture for her.

She was an early riser, he'd discovered. She'd been ready to shop when he awoke, destroying his breakfast-in-bed-with-a-rose-on-the-tray gambit. He'd looked up at her legs in a Nanna Bear skirt and instantly decided to add a short-short skirt to his line.

There was just something memorable about testing a mattress for fit with his new wife. About considering all the years they would spend making love on it. About lying down on the plastic-covered mattress and turning this way and that. About bouncing a bit to hear Jillian laugh and to catch the soft flow of her body against his for a heartbeat. He'd flopped over on her playfully, and one soft kiss had led to another. She'd flushed beautifully, her fingers shyly smoothing his chest, sensual tension humming between them.

After tucking his wife into bed and enduring a night of tossing on his lonely quilt, Cordell had fit his lips to hers. Their scorching kiss had embarrassed the furniture clerk. Jillian had wiggled away too quickly, and the look she shot down at him, filled with hunger and excitement, had helped soothe his unstable nerves and aching body.

Her speedy ability to balance his personal checking account frightened him. He wanted her to open her own account, but Jillian had insisted on transferring her checking account into his. She intended to pay her part of the household bills. That nettled his pride. He'd begun to notice a certain expression, the digging in of her womanly heels, when he didn't like the current project.

Not all phases of the furniture safari ran smoothly, but Cordell began to enjoy the adventure with his wife. She insisted on honesty. If he said that she could choose, Jillian's hurt look said he didn't care. He could fail The Test easily, with one wrong comment. Along about sofa-judging time, Cordell discovered that a neutral nod or a

"Hmm..." would lead into a war zone. He liked a big, angular wood-and-fabric couch, but Jillian preferred one that would make a nice "conversation area." The sectional, with its modern and curved design, would look fine in front of the fireplace.

"I can't sleep on something like that," Cordell stated flatly, because she had asked for complete honesty. "I'd be permanently bent."

"You don't like it." Jillian walked to a lamp and held it to the couch. She picked up a swatch set and began flipping through it. "You don't like it," she repeated, and an ominous shroud settled over Cordell. He knew he had wandered into a hazardous marital zone.

He shifted tactics. "Uh...I thought you said we might look for a cute little dressing table for you. One that women sit at and brush their hair at night. Before they come to bed. To their husbands."

She frowned at him. "That's for the bedroom. We're doing that when our time slot isn't so tight. Right now we have to be concerned with function, and what will look nice for our open house. What do you think about this fabric?"

"I like it," he said, certain that he had pleased her.

She peered over her glasses at him. "You're just saying that."

She made it sound as if he didn't care. He blankety-blank did care. He wanted her to be happy. But the swatch of material had pink in it. "A man doesn't like pink," he stated firmly, convinced that all men in America were on his side and would not sit upon pink.

"Oh, is that on a magazine poll, or etched in stone or something?" Jillian asked archly.

He didn't want to argue with her. He wanted everything in their nest to be just the way she wanted. "If you like it, it's okay."

"Mmm... That's a lukewarm statement if I ever heard one. What about beige?"

The beige lacked pink, and was the color of a horse he liked. "Great," Cordell said, and was pleased when Jillian nodded.

"They have a nice texture" was all he could think of when she showed him the modern pottery lamps.

She studied the lamps. "I'd rather have something more—"

"Why don't we think about it?" he asked with growing confidence. The shape of the lamps didn't matter, if they lit the room well. But it seemed important to Jillian. "If you like pottery, Mavis Lightfoot has a studio."

Jillian considered the lamps. "You like the natural look, don't you, Cordell?"

"I'd like to have a look that reflects us both, and the way we are becoming one," he said very carefully, watching her. He didn't want to be compared with Marsh, and he didn't want to use Jillian's talents for his benefit. He just wanted to cuddle Jillian and call her "dear heart" and make love to her.

She wanted to do so much too quickly. Eventually she'd run out of energy, and then she'd settle down into her wifely role—

Jillian moved to snuggle against him again. "That was so beautiful that I think I'm going to cry."

"Don't." Cordell held her very tightly, fearing that he had hurt her.

"I'm so happy." She burrowed deeper into his arms and rested her lips against his throat. "You're really trying, aren't you, honey bear?"

Her "honey bear" set him off. It drenched him in sunshine and filled him with warmth. Cordell drew her into the hanging-rugs section. Between an Oriental design and a modern one, he kissed her. She had the sweetest little tongue, agile and playful and... Cordell went taut as he realized that Jillian's rhythmic suckling of his tongue echoed the primitive throbbing in his loins.

He was becoming very aware of his loins, he decided instantly when she stepped back, looking cute and flustered. "I hope you didn't mind my instant reaction to you, Cordell. I don't want to frighten you, but sometimes I get urges that are beyond my understanding. They surpass hugs. They leap into—"

Cordell carefully placed his hands over her breasts and caressed her through the fine cotton sweater she wore. "Let's take the afternoon off and go back to camp," he heard himself offering huskily.

"We can't. We have Amanda's shower. There's the furniture people delivering furniture this afternoon, and I don't know what to wear. All I have is..." Jillian paused while Cordell kissed the corners of her lips. "...is my basic black cocktail dress, and things that don't look very—"

Cordell groaned slightly as his hands settled upon her hips. He squeezed the soft flesh gently, comforted that he hadn't dreamed the lush shape of her. "Amanda will understand."

Her hand reached to his forehead. "Cordell, I think you're running a fever. Are you?"

"I'll get an air mattress for under the sleeping bag," he whispered urgently against her throat. He dived into her feminine scents, wallowed in them for the first time that day.

"We have to get a thank-you card and a hostess gift for Amanda. We have little time to prepare for the open house. We have to get plants for the porch, maybe a swinging bench, lawn furniture for the outside barbecue... Cordell, you are making me very nervous. Grown-ups do not hide in the carpet and rug section and undress each other."

Cordell lifted and eased her farther back into the hanging rugs. "I don't want to sleep apart ever again."

"This is more complicated than I thought. We're going through a major adjustment—" Jillian caught her bottom lip between her teeth as Cordell slid his hand under her skirt, finding the elastic of her briefs.

"I've always liked good old elastic," he murmured as she began to tremble.

"Me too," she whispered against his throat, her hands clutching his shoulders as his fingers found her intimately. He took her cry into his mouth, aching wildly for her. Cordell rocked her against him, trembling with his rising desire as she was settling down from hers.

"What did you do?" she asked shakily, cuddling limply to him.

Cordell kissed her hair and rocked her in his arms. "Just a little thing someone told me about buttons. I never tried that before."

She squeezed him tighter. "You mean it? You only did that to me?"

He knew instantly that he had pleased her. Tonight he hoped to please her even more. He realized he was grinning. "Only you."

6

"Oh, sure. It doesn't matter what I wear," Jillian repeated as she glared at Cordell that evening. "You know how important first impressions are. These are *your* friends, Cordell. You know what to wear—polished boots, a dress shirt and slacks. I'm at a disadvantage. I've never been to a Wyoming get-together. What about palazzo pants? I've got a nice silk-vest-and-palazzo-pant outfit in batik. I don't want to wear your designs, because I want to separate work from play. Some of these people are employees. Why are you shaking your head? Don't you like batik?"

Seated on their new couch, Cordell pushed away an array of suit jackets and vests and a mountain of gauzy skirts and lacy sweaters. He looked disgruntled and tired and cornered. She had noted that a small quiver of distaste ran through him when she mentioned palazzo pants. Though he had stoically moved and rearranged the furniture to her pleasure, she wished he wouldn't keep answering her questions with a "Hmm..." a frown, and a nod. He seemed very noncommittal and a bit uncertain when she asked, "You're the designer. What should I wear?"

He shrugged and sank his jaw down into his collar. His expression was that of an Alamo defender—trying his best, but knowing that he couldn't win. "Wear that navy one with the pink roses."

"The print is too bold. I'll think of something, if you just don't keep interfering."

"I thought you wanted my input. You asked," Cordell reminded her, definitely uncertain now. There was nothing uncertain about the way he had issued threats to his male friends when he thought she wasn't listening. They were reluctant to go to the shower, too, wanting to hole up at the town pool hall until time to pick up their wives. "Be there," Cordell had growled during several calls, "or I'll share some interesting secrets about our last hunting trip."

Jillian had no idea men could act so threatened when attending a wedding shower. "I'll make up my own mind about what I wear, thank you very much. I can't go," she said finally, collapsing in a defeated heap beside him on their brand-new couch. She tucked his long, soft chambray shirt around her thighs. She loved wearing his clothing, wrapping his scent around her. "I don't have anything to wear. I've flunked the new-wife test. No soft little sweet-bride prints in my entire wardrobe."

"I'm not any damned up-and-coming corporate-ladder-climbing hotshot who needs his wife prettying up for the crowd and running interference for him," Cordell said firmly after a moment. "You think you've got problems... We're going to a friend's house. We'll be with friends, and there damned well better be men there."

Though his tone was angry, his fingers stroked the tense nape of her neck gently. "You smell good."

"Oh, it's the soap," she returned automatically, realizing that none of her clothes suited rural Wyoming. She allowed Cordell to draw her into his arms. Then upon his lap. She stroked the space between his eyebrows, the special piece of skin she adored, though he had glorious skin everywhere. "All I have is basic black mix-and-match and palazzo pants."

She settled into his gentle nuzzling kisses along her cheek and nestled her head against his shoulder. He kissed her lips, and she wrapped her arms around him. Cordell smoothed her bare thigh and trembled a bit, his fingers sliding beneath her lacy briefs to stroke her. "We could stay at home."

She shook her head. "Amanda will have gone to so much trouble...." She gave herself to Cordell's hungry kisses, gasped when he suckled at her breast and shot to the heavens when he touched her *there*. She wilted into a relaxed heap, content to be stroked and cuddled and kissed. "I'm better now. Not so nervous," she whispered shakily against his rumpled hair.

"Hey. What are husbands for?" he asked unevenly, handing her a hot-pink batik jacket and a basic black skirt. The dark, promising hunger in his eyes didn't reflect his light tone. She knew that he wanted her desperately. That he found her attractive in an old shirt.

Later, when they arrived at Amanda's, she noted that Cordell circled the ranch house with his pickup, as if scouting the lay of the land. "What's wrong?" she asked.

"There better be men here," he repeated for the tenth time, looking very wary.

"Where's the card?"

He looked down at her with a blank expression. "The card?"

"The one to thank Amanda. The one to go with the hostess gift I got. Remember, Cordell? We ran short of time, and you were to pick out the card while I got the gift."

"What did you get?" he asked, and she knew he was playing for time.

Jillian fluffed the ribbons on the wrapped gift. "A *latte* maker. I hope she doesn't have one. You forgot the card, didn't you?"

"Every dirt-poor rancher sure needs a good *latte* maker.... Cards are scary," he admitted after a time, and a muscle in his jaw contracted and released. "There were too many. I don't do cards."

"Cordell!" She took the small envelope he handed her and opened it. Thanks, the plain white card read. He hadn't signed it. He hadn't linked their names together as if they were one. The neglect cut her to the heart. "You didn't sign our names," she whispered sadly.

Cordell scowled down at her. "If we hand it to her, she'll know it's from us. She can reuse it," he stated indignantly.

"I did my part, Cordell," she reminded him, aching for their unsigned names and the way he'd forgotten to link them in writing for the world to see.

"Is this an important event in our lives, me not signing the card?" he asked warily, beginning to understand his crime. He quickly said, "I just didn't have time. Let me do it now."

Their names, linked together in Cordell's big bold scrawl, pacified her, and she snuggled closer. Cordell tugged her into his arms. The wrapped *latte* maker wedged space between them as he lowered her back to the seat. Paper tore as he reached to find her breast—

Amanda jerked open the pickup door, grinning down at them along with a herd of other grins. A small girl pushed through the mob to peer at Jillian. The girl's missing front tooth caused a lisp as she said, "So this is the one who finally trapped him."

Cordell leaned past Jillian and kissed the little girl's cheek. "I was waiting for you, rosebud. But this one bushwhacked me."

At the party, Cordell acted very old-fashioned and proud of his wife. Jillian instantly detected that the few men attending had been forced to come. They huddled together and glared at Cordell, who looked as if he needed their protection. He was just making his getaway to the males on the front porch when Jillian nabbed him. He stopped in his tracks as she stepped in front of him.

"You're deserting me," she whispered, wanting him at her side.

"The men are on the porch." He levered the statement into the air between them like a stone.

"You didn't act this way at your rehearsal-reception," she persisted, hurt by his small act of desertion.

"I was afraid the Cling-ons would get you, and your family isn't exactly sweet. Everyone here is my friend. You'll be fine."

Refusing to be put off, Jillian eyed him. "I am your bride, alone in a new land. Oh, fine. Just run off and hide."

Cordell shook his head and ran his hand through his hair, clearly considering the current marriage disaster. He glanced longingly at the men outside on the porch. He looked warily at the excited women hovering over the newly unwrapped household gifts. Jillian waited for him to choose, crying inside as the heartbeats stretched into a full minute.

"You're right," Cordell said finally, slipping his arm around her waist and drawing her close to him. "Don't ever forget that I won't fail you when you need me," he said, as if going off to war because of her.

He was sweet, trying to find something exciting about dish towels and pillowcases. He tried so hard that Jillian let him escape to the other men, who were engrossed in the *latte* machine.

When they drove home, intoxicated a bit by the glowing, dreamy expressions at the shower, Cordell pulled off the road. The moon filtered through the pine trees as he turned to her. The air between them was scented of best wishes and Amanda's party. Jillian met his kisses hungrily, and Cordell was just moving over her when Nanna appeared with her flashlight. "Thought it was rustlers. Nice party, huh?"

Cordell's mood darkened immediately, and his passion dampened. His terse answers to her tentative make-nice questions were almost growls.

When Jillian decided to follow her instincts and step into his shower, she found Cordell standing beneath the icy-cold water, his fists balled. He was muttering darkly. Clearly she had interrupted a private-summit meeting of an enraged male in his cave. He glared at her through the streaming water and snapped, "What?" flatly. Cordell grabbed her before she could step out, and whispered urgently, "Hold on to me."

"You're too big.... This is an awful idea. We don't fit." Desperation ran through her now.

He sheltered her from the icy blast with his body. He looked glorious with water streaming down his head, spraying over it to reach her face. It bounced over his broad shoulders and streamed down the dark hair on his chest. "I'm up for new ideas," he whispered rawly as the water warmed and his hands cupped her buttocks, lifting her slightly.

"Water conservation," she explained reasonably, as he nudged open her legs and placed himself within her care. The incredible sweetness of allowing her to hold him intimately caused her to blush.

As Cordell nudged deeper, she trembled and locked her fingers on to the safety of his shoulders. He stood very still, waiting for her to touch him. She explored his chest, soaped it slowly, her eyes holding his. He touched her wet hair, her cheeks, her lips and lowered his mouth to hers. He slid gently inside her, and whispered rawly, "We fit just fine."

They'd missed the entire shivaree, the hooting and honking and fireworks outside, she discovered later as she snuggled in Cordell's arms before the fireplace. "Let's go to bed, darling," Cordell whispered against her ear, his hand caressing her breast.

Jillian bit her lip, not wanting to refuse him—her brand-new husband who fit into the shower very nicely. Yet she couldn't live through the separation that would follow, if her talent and her working-woman tendencies weren't for Cordell. She wanted them to be friends and lovers. The balance was essential to her, and she wasn't certain she could maintain what she truly wanted, once on a marriage bed with Cordell.

Nanna appeared, and Cordell refused to let Jillian slide from his lap. Instead, he tugged the quilt around them and held her, while Nanna settled into the rocking chair and talked about the party and the shivaree—an event to celebrate the newlyweds. Jillian yawned and cuddled up to Cordell, who kept his hand firmly upon her breast beneath the quilt. She sensed that Nanna needed to know that their marriage was safe, that Cordell was happy—it was rather like putting her grandson to bed and tucking him in—and so Jillian listened to Cordell's rumbling voice and Nanna's rough whispers as she dozed. When Cordell thought she was asleep, he kissed her cheek and whispered to Nanna, "She's real cute, isn't she? You should see her when she gets riled, all fire and woman. Makes me go weak. Sometimes the sun glints off her hair and her lashes and she looks just like an angel. Unless she's mad. Then she looks hot as a chili pepper, and passion-ripe."

Jillian was elated as she heard Cordell's description of her to his grandmother. She allowed her lips to brush his skin as a reward. He tasted of her soap and their love-making. He made love gloriously, as if every inch of her delighted him. She nuzzled his shoulder again, confident that the future would smooth out into a straight, harmonious road for a lifetime.

Nanna puffed on her pipe. "You're drooling, boy. Do you think I'll get any grandkids out of her?"

"Wouldn't be surprised, old woman. She'd make a real sweet mama. She's been pretty nervous, so don't count on it soon. Heifers usually have to settle down a bit first."

Heifers?

"You're the cautious kind, and you're planning a family with this one, when the others didn't matter. Did you have her tested to see if she's the mama kind?"

"No need to. I just knew that everything was natural between us. We fit when it counts. She's mine now, and everything will work out fine. Maybe a little girl or two to keep her busy. Or there might be little stray mavericks that need adopting."

Jillian held very still, suddenly awake. She hadn't thought of herself as a heifer, which she knew was an unbred young cow. She realized that they hadn't talked about having children—other than that they both liked them—and that Cordell had made *their* most important life decision by himself. She had planned to launch Nanna Bear successfully, showing Cordell who and what she was—a competitive, talented and independent player. She wanted him to know who she was deep down in her bones, so that there would only be truth between them. From there they could build a relationship. She wouldn't turn her back again on what lurked within her. She had explained to him who and what she was, but he didn't take her seriously.

Nanna winked at Jillian, who was frowning now as Cordell continued to rock her. "So you just swooped into New York and plucked a cute little baby doll out, did you? A little wifey you can take care of, fix things for, and who's just going to love staying at home, while you're out there in the big bad world, taking the knocks and making a living."

Cordell's chin nudged the top of Jillian's head as he nodded. "That's what women want. Portia and Alicia liked the arrangement, but women can get tricky when you live separately. You'd never believe what Portia— No, never mind, I don't want to think about modern technology. Women take care of the social stuff—it's best if the roles are clearly defined, though I did get the thank-you card today," he stated proudly, as if he had swum the English Channel. "Just to help her out until she settles in. Jillian is an old-fashioned girl. She'll get in the flow of the wife business soon enough."

"Is that right? Some women like to be partners, you know, boy. They like a thing called an equal relationship. Some of them like working outside the nest, you know. But you seem to have all the thinking sorted about this marriage already. So you finally got you a winner, huh?" Nanna persisted softly. "I hear that she's got the plant stirred up. Seems like she's a whiz, a real go-getter."

"She won't have to worry her pretty little head about anything." Cordell nuzzled Jillian's curls and rocked her gently. Jillian held very still. He was just tossing her a pacifier when he said she could bring home the bacon.

Bacon. Pork. Chauvinist pig.

"She'll settle down," Cordell continued confidently. "It's just bridal nerves and energy. She did lay out a good plan, though. The best I've ever seen. I'll play along until she gets tired of the idea and decides to take the traditional woman's role in the marriage. She'll take care of her part, and I'll see that she's happy. I'll hire someone to see her ideas through, and that will be enough for her— Hey!" he yelled as Jillian locked her fingers into his chest hair and tugged.

"You let anyone else into my campaign, buddy, and you'll see that this little baby doll can play dirty pool." Jillian grabbed the quilt to her and left him sitting nude on the couch. He rubbed his chest and jammed a pillow over his lap. Nanna's roaring laughter continued after Jillian slammed the bedroom door closed.

Cordell lingered outside his studio, gripping his coffee cup as if it were a lifeline. His unhappy bride had apparently been working since dawn. He braced himself, tried to shake out the kinks created by the curved couch, and gripped the studio doorknob. He inhaled once, then turned the knob.

There she was, his happy little homemaker, his bride. Dressed in her backward ball cap, wearing a Nanna Bear blouse and a pair of worn cutoff overalls with pencils and pens stashed in the pockets. The toe of one worn running shoe tapped his clean studio floor. He prayed that no scraps or notes had been lost during the cleaning-massacre. She had rearranged furniture, yet his drawing table remained in the same well-lit area. His table was cluttered, as usual, next to his bulletin board, which was tacked with fabric and sketches. He appreciated the consideration since everything else in his life was rearranged. Ace was talking with her, his expression animated, as they leaned over a selection of photographs. Cordell clutched his sketchbook closer, the one with his nightgown design and his little girls' dresses. The firmly closed bedroom door had provided hours of sketching time. He'd failed to get her the breakfast tray again, and the refrigerator rose was looking aged. He drew out his pocket notebook and wrote, "New rose."

His father had handed his mother a huge bouquet of wildflowers. *I'm just sorry they aren't roses, dear heart.*

You're my rose, Cordell's mother had whispered, tears in her eyes.

Cordell shook his head, startled by the memory. He swallowed the emotion humming through him. His parents had never looked at each other without love; even their arguments hadn't been bitter.

"Oh, Cordell. I'm glad you're here," Jillian said, as if just noticing him. She moved toward him, the light gleaming on her legs. Cordell shifted back from the images, pushing them away.

He remembered how those legs had wrapped around him in the shower as they conserved water. She brushed a kiss against his cheek and held his hand in the reassuring way he liked. "How do you like the changes, honey?"

Honey. She'd called him "honey." Cordell's tension eased. She wasn't mad at him anymore. He released his trapped breath and caught it again when he noted the slightly dark shade of her eyes behind her lenses. He studied her closely. A tinge of mad remained.

Jillian handed him several pages of faxes. "Harry's résumé. The accountant I was telling you about. He's anxious to come and can be here tomorrow. It's up to you. He is good."

"I like doing the books," Cordell said warily, feeling his kingdom being invaded.

"What do you like about it? I thought you might like the time to create, or do something else."

She was watching him carefully, and he knew that she expected him to fill in the blanks. They loomed before him, waiting to be filled. "I like seeing profit," he answered truthfully. "It's been growing steadily."

He realized he had failed to fill in the blanks when she said, too softly, "We need time together."

"Oh. I draw in the morning." Drawing sketches was a safe zone, and Cordell plunged into it, searching for a successful recovery. Cordell eased into his chair and began to work on his sketches as Ace and Jillian returned to the photographs. Periodically she wandered over to him and rested against him, her hand smoothing his shoulder. He really needed those little caresses in his unstable world. He missed his fish, his goose and his antlers, now hanging in a shed.

Why hadn't he remembered the love between his parents? There had always been that love running through their lives, despite the bad times.

"Do you like what I'm wearing?" she asked softly as he drew her closer, her hips between his legs, so that they could study his designs together.

Another memory locked on to him, one of his mother asking his father that same question. Cordell shivered at the pain, and turned his attention to his wife.

She needed comforting, just as he did, he thought, encircling her with his arms and resting his cheek along hers. "I like you," he whispered honestly, wishing Ace would stop muttering about shutter speeds and bad light.

"Do you? The working-woman side of me?"

Too late, Cordell realized he was in a war zone, the bomb was ticking and the pressure was on.

Amanda saved him, her voice spitting from the intercom. "Jillian, take line two. Some woman named Buffy is having a hissy fit."

Cordell tightened his arms around his wife. The Clingons were after her. If they dragged her back into their bog— "Cordell, everything will be fine. Stop crushing me," Jillian murmured. She allowed his fist to grip the back straps of her overalls as she picked up the telephone. "Hello, Buffy... Yes, I can call you Mother.... That's a good start.... Yes, Grandma is a little hard to swallow— It's your choice. What about Grammy? Like in the awards? You could picture yourself a star."

Cordell looked at his white knuckles as he gripped her straps, and Jillian sent him a look over her shoulder. She wiggled free and frowned as she spoke. "Cordell is a marvelous husband.... Yes, he's a little heavy-handed at times and he's prone to takeovers."

Speaking quietly, Jillian turned away from him. "Mother. Yes, I know about the orphanage."

She glanced warily at Cordell. "Yes, I would imagine that he was listed as hardheaded and a fighter. Do not ever again investigate the man I love. Never. Ever. No, Cordell is not considering anything of the kind. He's not going to sign an exclusive contract with Horton's. I'm working on his marketing plan. What? You talked to his ex-wife and Alicia? You actually asked about his—?"

The toe of her jogger tapped the swept boards, and Cordell shifted uneasily as Jillian leveled a dark stare at him over her glasses. "Cordell is not sexually impaired.

I don't care what either of them says. He's not a brute, a throwback or a mountain man, and Portia is dead wrong. Cordell is not unimaginative when he makes love," she declared hotly before continuing, "I have *not* been subjugated and brainwashed.... He does not beat me. He has not given me stock, or anything else, for a wedding present."

Cordell clenched a length of lace. *He'd forgotten to give his bride a wedding gift...just like he'd forgotten to sign the card.*

"I'm wearing his mother's ring, and that's enough." Jillian's low tone had taken on a touch of defensive anger. Cordell was uneasy with his wife's having cause to defend him; the p's and q's of marriage weren't easy, he decided as he listened to her. "No, he's not using me for my ability or for my family connections. I have experience with Marsh, remember? I'd know a user. Cordell is my husband, and we're just fine. No, he isn't trying to get me barefoot and pregnant. No, I did not punch holes in his prevention.... How's the mothering business going?" Jillian tossed a bone to her mother, changing subjects.

Cordell glanced at Ace, who was peering at him over the photograph litter. Ace's expression had a big tsk-tsk-you-failed written on it. "Out," Cordell ordered.

"Mother, I won't forget to call. Take care of yourself and the family." Jillian replaced the telephone and looked out the studio window to the sprawling pines and rugged mountains. "I miss them," she whispered when Cordell came to stand behind her. "It was good to talk with Mother."

Cordell hesitated, certain that just a moment before, Jillian had not been happy to talk with Buffy. Jillian reached behind her, found his hands and drew his arms around her. "Hold me."

His mother had moved into his father's arms just that same way. *I love you, dear heart,* his father had whispered. Pain caught Cordell's heart, the sudden memory jarring him. The hidden memories had erupted suddenly on their wedding night. Why?

Cordell pushed his insecurities and his worry about the lack of a proper wedding gift for his bride away and held her. After a time, Jillian turned and burrowed against his chest, and he stroked her hair. His wife was loyal to those she loved. She sniffed and wiped her eyes on his collar. "I really miss them, and they miss me. It wasn't until I was divorced that I realized that I loved fixing the family problems. Tiffany has maxed out her credit cards. George needs me to soothe ruffled business feathers. Mother has no idea about being supportive if it doesn't net her a villa in Italy or five-carat jewelry. They're so helpless in a way, and it's a struggle for them to solve family problems without me. There were times that I actually helped save the company from bankruptcy. I miss that. I enjoy being inventive."

"I don't want you for your talent or your family connections." Cordell repeated her statement firmly. "I want to take care of you. I want to make you happy. It's just that the ground is a little shaky at times."

Jillian gripped the front of his shirt. "You're doing just fine, Cordell. But we have to relate more. You really haven't expressed any inner feelings to me. I realize that takes time and we're in a crunch—"

"Why are we in a crunch?" He wondered what train had run over him. Was she leaving him?

"Marketing is based on timing. Spring designs sell well. We have to be there with the goods, and we're running late."

"Let's go to bed," he offered, wanting to soothe her in the only way he knew would relax her. He also wanted to reassure himself that their lovemaking had happened and wasn't a dream. She'd given herself to him totally, without reservation, the emotion stunning him. Jillian was so beautiful when she went limp, just after her eyes widened with that intimate feminine pleasure.

She blinked up at him. "Cordell, do you find me sexually satisfying?"

He thought about Portia's appliance and countered, "Do I satisfy you?"

"There's more to marriage than sex. We're building a relationship based on truth, aren't we?"

He thought about things he didn't want anyone to know—his fears of failure. He knew his scars were based on the hardships of his youth and the lean years with his grandmother. She'd sacrificed for him, and never complained. He feared that somehow something would go wrong and he wouldn't be able to protect or care for those he loved, Nanna and his friends who worked for him. "I don't want you to worry," he stated slowly, finding the words uneasily. "You've been raised with money, and I'll provide for you."

Jillian went very still and looked up at him. She touched his cheek, and his mother's wedding ring glittered a myriad of colors across her face. "You're not going to fail, Cordell. Neither am I. We're a twosome. Equal partners, in the bad and the good."

Then she walked out the door.

* * *

On a cutting table, Jillian tucked the photo-layout mock-up into a large black carrying case. She zipped it up and looked around the deserted building. Nanna Bear workers could bring plants and photos for their work areas—some employers wouldn't allow the clutter. They were happy to be going home now, back to their gardens and ranches. The rural community needed Cordell as much as he needed them. They were his family, and he worried about them.

During the day, he had yelled at her for climbing a ladder with the photographer, and she had yelled back. The instant Cordell placed his boot on the ladder, she'd realized she'd made a mistake. He'd been worried about her, but being unceremoniously retrieved and dangling by her back straps from Cordell's big fist was not the executive marketing image she wanted. A roaring lecture about her safety in front of the Nanna Bear workers had embarrassed and shocked her. No one, not even her father, had ever yelled at her. Censure was done in quiet, clinical and deadly cuts. *Dingbat* was not a word that had ever applied to her. She had always been realistic. That was probably why she'd launched a pot of violets at him. Cordell had caught it and slammed it into a sewing machine.

The entire staff had watched, their expressions a little dreamy, as though they were remembering their first days at marriage. "Kiss her, Cordell," Oren Long hooted.

Jillian had stepped back from the instant predatory gleam in Cordell's black eyes. "Don't you dare!"

He'd taken another step, looming over her. "Who's going to stop me?"

"Threats?" Jillian had inhaled, narrowed her eyes and suppressed the urge to run. She'd lifted her chin, adjusted her ball cap firmly and held her ground. "Listen, buddy of mine. Do it and you'll be sorry. Kisses—the way you deliver them—are a private thing."

Cordell had stood back and folded his arms over his chest. The tilt of his head had been all male arrogance, not giving an inch. "You owe me a good one later, then. A real good lip-sucking, sweet little purring one."

"I don't feel like bargaining. No one has ever—ever—in my entire lifetime hauled me around like a child. Nor has anyone called me a 'dingbat.' Until now. Until you."

Now, Jillian arched and stretched, weary after the long day. She wanted Cordell to hold her. She wished she hadn't lost her temper and called him an overbearing brute. Cordell was the only man in her lifetime to cause her to lose her temper. She wished she hadn't kicked him in the shin when he grabbed her overalls' straps and began hauling her toward the door. Watching him limp away, his shoulders taut with anger, had reached right into the guilty core of her.

Jillian trudged up to the studio to turn off the lights. Standing at the open door, she saw Cordell bent over his sketching table, the floor littered with balls of paper and fabric, and the adjustable light gleaming in his rumpled hair. The angles of his face caught the shadows. He paused periodically, as if going inside, to his creative well, and fishing for ideas. The quick slash-slash of his pencil echoed in the darkened room. Fascinated, Jillian set aside the carrying case, locked the door against the world and came to his side.

Absorbed in his work, Cordell didn't move as she studied him. The beam outlined his tall body against the shadows, the sweep of his shoulders, the tapering of his body into those long legs. Jillian breathed quietly, her heart racing. This magnificent creature was hers to tend, to soothe. Cordell battled a darkness within him, closing himself off from her at times. She hoped that as he grew to trust her with his past, he would share that life with her. It had forged much of his behavior and attitudes, and she needed to understand. She eased between Cordell and his sketch table and smoothed the creases on his forehead with her fingertips. He looked at her warily.

"I'm sorry I kicked you." She was beginning to understand primitive behavior, when it related to one's mate.

"I'm working on new designs, a bias-cut skirt..." His lips responded to her light kiss. "You also yelled at me."

"I refuse to take all the blame. You yelled first." Jillian deepened the kiss, fitting her mouth to his. Cordell's large hands circled her waist instantly. "I want you," she whispered, aching for him. She opened her mouth and gave him what he wanted, moved restlessly as his hands shed the overalls from her.

She tore away his shirt and loosened the belt of his jeans, the fire rising in her. Cordell's large body shivered as she bore him down to the floor and straddled him.

He looked so lusciously male, his hair tousled by her fingers, his jaw rough with stubble and his nipples peaking when she licked them. Cordell groaned when she took him deep inside, to the very depths of her femininity and need.

His hands found and locked on to her bottom, urging her on until she collapsed, shaking, upon him. "You're mine, a part of me, my heart, my love," she remembered whispering urgently sometime during the storm.

Rallying slightly to reality, Jillian glanced down at their torn clothing, the way Cordell's jeans were tangled around his ankles. She flushed and tried to squirm away, embarrassed by her primitive need of him.

Cordell kept her securely attached to him. "Let's try this again, dear heart," he whispered, his caress skimming across her breasts.

The second time they made love, she heard the echo of her cry, even as she began to dissolve.

Cordell laughed aloud when she grumbled, protesting his carrying her into the small, functional bathroom. He turned on the shower faucets and began to undress her. "I'm sorry, Cordell. I don't know what possessed me. It was just like...there you were, my special dessert... Here we are at our place of business, and I..."

"You keep thinking that way. Just remember that turnabout is fair play."

Cordell soaped and washed her thoroughly; then, while she dried, he stepped into the shower. Regretting that they'd wasted so much water in separate showers, she slipped into Cordell's shirt and wandered out to the darkened studio. The papers and cloth were scattered and flattened in their lovemaking place, evidence of her need for her husband. She picked them up and straightened them, shocked by what she had done.

He came to stand behind her, rocking her in his arms as they looked out over the twinkling lights of the town and the sprawling mountains. "We'll invite your family here," Cordell said finally. "They need to know that you're safe."

"They'll make your life miserable. You don't know how to take them...that when they say something uncaring, they may feel something else. It's a family trait."

"You didn't inherit it, and you'll take care of me," he returned, gathering her closer. "I'm sorry I yelled at you today," he repeated, and she knew it was important to him that she understood.

"You were frightened, weren't you?" She remembered his expression the instant before he'd turned into a raging tyrant. Cordell had been stricken with terror, afraid that she would fall.

"No one has ever thrown a plant at me before." She allowed him to change the subject; she knew he was afraid. Cordell lifted her in his arms and carried her to the couch. "Stay put."

Jillian snuggled down into Cordell's shirt. She preferred honest yelling with him to the quiet, civilized deadly barbs of her family and Marsh.

With a towel wrapped around his hips, Cordell looked into the tiny refrigerator. He retrieved cheese and crackers and bottles of mineral water and came to sit beside her. "You're a primitive woman, dear heart. A real takeover artist."

"I jumped you. Ambushed you while you were working... Oh, Cordell, I had you on the floor...." she muttered, still horrified at the need that had enveloped her like fire. "Don't talk about it. I am truly horrified."

"Gets better and better," Cordell murmured smugly, as if his decision to lasso and brand her as his own were working right on schedule. He placed crackers and cheese between her lips. "We just have to work out the fine points."

Jillian hoped that Cordell's fine points were the same issues as hers. "Any pizza-delivery places around Slough Foot? I'm dying for a carton of good fried Chinese noodles.... Cordell, please don't think that I am criticizing all the wonderful work you've done so far in marketing Nanna Bear. I'm trying to be helpful."

When he went very still, Jillian knew that her intuition had scored a bull's-eye.

7

At six o'clock the next morning, Cordell watched his wife jog toward him. His mission was to waylay her before she got to work. He'd made a mistake by hesitating when she asked him about his feelings. He wasn't used to sharing his life or his business. He'd cuddle her, try to get her into bed and keep her there. Though Jillian had allowed him to hold her on the couch last night, they'd both been tense and wary. He ached from her elbows and knees—especially from the time her knee had unintentionally knifed him in his... On their bed, he'd have more room to show her that he cared. Elbows and knees and chins and legs would have more room to fit together.

Her ponytail caught the sunrise as she passed through the lofty pines. Her pink neon shorts and knit top showed every curve. He liked the cut of the shorts, which allowed him to glimpse the lower curve of her bottom. He appreciated the feminine muscles on her legs, and just watching her, he went taut. He placed the fresh rose between his teeth and eased out the door, carrying the morning herbal tea she preferred, his coffee, and a buttered croissant in each of his shirt pockets.

With her ponytail bobbing as she ran in place, cooling down, Jillian grinned at him. "Hi. You look good in rose."

He drooled as he noted the sweat-darkened area between her breasts. This was his precious wife, the woman he wanted to protect and pamper. "Let's sit down on the porch, enjoy the morning and each other," Cordell invited boldly around the rose. He glanced at the spacious new padded bench on the front porch.

Jillian followed his line of vision and immediately launched herself against him, crushing the croissants in his pockets. Her arms locked around his neck and her tongue eased over the thornless rose stem to neatly comfort his. He realized that he was standing, legs braced, holding a cup in each hand, while his wife's long legs wrapped around his hips. Cordell backed to the porch bench and gently lowered onto it, setting the hot liquid aside as Jillian tried new and interesting angles to kiss him around the rose.

Cordell filled his palms with her bottom and forgot his plan to waylay her. Fifteen minutes later, he lay draped across the bench, floating in a huge grin that covered his entire body. Jillian eased away from him, kissed him sweetly and smoothed his rumpled hair. She kissed him again, nuzzled his cheek with hers as he caressed her nude breast. Jillian tucked the crushed rose between his lips again and kissed him. "Love you," she whispered tenderly before she rose, drew her bra up over her breasts and sipped her cooled tea. She tugged her T-shirt from his limp hand and jogged into the house.

Cordell inhaled the fresh, chilly May air and continued to float. So much for enticing her into bed. He eased all the way out of his shirt, the squashed croissants buttering his chest.

He waited for her exclamation of surprise and delight. The brand-new home computer awaited her in a small room off the kitchen. He'd carefully cut out footprints to lead her to it. Jillian's happy cry launched him to his feet. He tucked the rose behind his ear, close at hand, for when Jillian discovered how much he cared. A happy marriage awaited him—with luck, he'd make it into her bedroom this morning, afternoon and evening. He didn't bother to snap his jeans or replace his shirt.

Cordell blinked as he remembered their frantic, tropical encounter on the front porch. After she kissed him around the rose, his plan to ease her into bed went awry in a mass of quickly shed clothing. He rubbed his bare chest and thought about how neatly Jillian's newly buttered breasts slid against him.

"This is so thoughtful of you, honey," Jillian exclaimed, seated at the computer and punching buttons, quickly running through its capabilities. She beamed up at him, looking all cute and curvy in her bra and briefs.

He glowed internally. He had pleased his mate. Husbanding was a cinch.

"We can really use this now, especially when we're in this crunch to get the house set up for the business party. I think we'll make the smallest bedroom into an office. We'll need a fax— Oh, great! This computer has faxing capability. Cordell, you are wonderful! A home office away from the plant will help prevent distractions." She frowned, punching into more programs. "What's this? A genealogy program and a recipe program? I didn't know you were interested in either one."

He smiled weakly, his hopes crumbling upon his bare, cold feet. Jillian's agile little toes and arches might not be warming his tomorrow morning in bed.

Her eyes widened slightly. "Cordell? *Are* you interested in genealogy and recipes?"

He could either lie to her or—

"They're for me, aren't they?" Jillian said after the May sunshine drew a line between them. That small line of gold between them resembled the one drawn at the OK Corral before the shoot-out.

Cordell locked his bare soles on the linoleum floor. Relating to a woman wasn't that easy. He hadn't noticed that before. Get a woman a gift, and you placed yourself out on a limb. Women asked tricky questions. He opted for a marriage based on truths. "I'd like kids with you. A whole houseful. The genealogy and the recipe programs could be useful. You know, to pass on family traditions from one generation to another. A reference for any genetic inheritances and traditions," he said after a moment, because it was true and because everything else was crumbling between them.

He tried for a safe subject, one that might distract her back to business. They seemed to be compatible in that area. "I've been thinking about designing a maternity line."

She rose slowly and faced him. "Does the Tarzan trait run in the males of the Dougald family?"

"What's that supposed to mean?"

"You Tarzan, me Jane. I have my place keeping the little cave homey and the kettle brewing and you drag home the dinosaur roast? You read too many Dick and Jane books, Cordell. You know, where Dick goes off to work and Jane plays Mrs. Cleaver, getting the Beaver and Wally off to school. After that, she cooks the Tyrannosaurus rex, cleans the rocks and goes on mind-hold until the hubby and kids turn up.... Take a note, Mr. Dougald. I am not Jane, or Mrs. Cleaver."

A chill shot through him. She didn't like his perfect gift.

In a huff, she brushed by him on her way to the bedroom. "But I am a woman who needs to exfoliate badly before she goes to work."

Cordell recovered, snapped the waistband of his jeans and reached the bedroom door just as it slammed in his face. "What was that about loving me?" he yelled.

"I do, you talented, thickheaded Neanderthal jerk."

He considered that. She always told the truth, except for that awful lie about Bomber's death. But the fine-tuning of the Dougalds' personal relationship was tricky. Women were very quirky. "Well. That's good. That's okay. I can deal with that," he muttered, and jerked the battered rose from over his ear.

He shook his head and wondered what had hit him. He rubbed his buttered chest and wondered what she had to exfoliate and when he was ever getting his wife into bed.

Or if her exfoliation project had anything to do with leaving him.

"I am normally a calm, reliable person. I *used* to be an emotional rock. I have never, ever yelled at anyone but Cordell Dougald." Jillian had worked feverishly at the plant, calling the printers to see if the invitations were ready; they were a combined declaration of marriage and of Nanna Bear's new leap into a bigger market. She'd edited the descriptions in the catalog and bullied the printer into working overtime to turn out the sample catalog copies. With the help of the office computer, she had quickly put together a first sampler. The glossy version would come later.

Cordell hadn't discovered her ugliest secret: she thrived on pressure. She loved the little problems that turned up in marketing, loved fashioning the temporary rough spots into successful coups.

She also loved Cordell. Could he cope with who she really was? She sucked on a pencil and looked at the spectacular scenery and thought about how delectable he'd looked coming toward her with cups in hand, croissants tucked in his pockets. She hadn't meant to jump him, but she couldn't trust herself in the vicinity of Cordell. Her primitive sexual need of him shocked her; also shocking was the way she could yell at him. Every throbbing emotion in her lifetime had been safely tucked away, until her maddening husband caused her to erupt.

Cordell had dark secrets of his own that he hoarded away from her. Shadows crossed his expressions and fear and carelessless somehow derived from fate. But when they were locked together, one body and one heart beating wildly together, Cordell was all hers. She would build upon that knowledge.

She shivered and remembered the episode on the front porch. The rose between his teeth had been a real challenge, and she'd always been a sucker for a challenge.

She couldn't settle for less than a well-rounded lifetime relationship. She couldn't allow Cordell to spend the night with her in bed, because she'd never let him go.

He'd run all over her, protecting her, pampering her, patting her on the head before he went out into the jungle to bring home the bacon. She dismissed the knowledge that it might be warthog, rather than plain pig bacon. The plus to having advertising talent was that she could bypass realities.

But Cordell was reality. Jillian held very still and allowed her deepest fear to enfold her in a cold, swirling mist. Could Cordell be on the rebound from his latest wife-replacement caper, with Alicia? Had Jillian snatched him for her own when he was most vulnerable?

At times Cordell tensed almost painfully, bound by something she didn't understand. What burdens tortured him when the dark moments came unexpectedly?

Cordell arrived just then, bursting through the studio door, six feet three inches of glorious, scowling cowboy. He shoved a huge bouquet of roses at her, bent to kiss her lips and said roughly, "You look good, darling. I was wrong. You were right. I guess that just about says it, huh?"

She hugged the roses, fighting tears. She mourned the battered rose that had been tucked over his ear. "Cordell, you have absolutely no idea of what went wrong this morning, do you?"

His frown deepened and turned wary. His neck sunk lower in his shirt collar, and she caught a glimpse of the little boy orphaned long ago. "I hope the exfoliating business went okay."

"I hurt your feelings, didn't I? You can tell me. Relate. Go ahead. There you were, all proud of your surprise, and I ruined it. I hurt you."

"Hurt?" he asked, as if the word had been spoken in an alien language and he was trying to understand. "Ah, dear heart...do you think you've been working too hard?" he asked slowly.

She stared at him, her husband, the man she was about to kiss. Her pucker tightened into a line. It eased again when Cordell lifted her hand to his lips, kissing her palm. "You're doing a spiffy job, dear heart."

That stopped her. She melted inside, softening toward the man who was looking down at her tenderly. Her glow sprung into a hopeful smile. "You think so?"

"I think you're right. We need to make time for ourselves."

"We've got the open house and the new line and the catalog...."

Cordell locked the studio door and gathered her into his arms. "I need a hug."

He needed her. All her womanly senses tilted as Cordell began to kiss her temple, the tip of her nose, her ear. His hard thigh slid between hers, nudging her gently. He fit his hands over her denim-covered backside and lifted her to him.

Jillian locked her arms around him and snuggled her face into his throat. "Everything will work out. You'll see."

That afternoon, Cordell slammed into the studio, jammed his hands onto his hips and glared at her. The lace tied around his forehead, bandito-style, emphasized his bold dark looks. An eyelet scrap clung to the hair on his chest; his shirt was open down to his tooled western belt. Another scrap of rosebud-spattered material swung from his jeans pocket. "You said everything will work out. Well, it isn't. We're out of chambray, and the suppliers say it will take a full ten days to get here. The seamstresses' husbands have lodged a complaint about work causing too much stress on their sex life. You started this mess in high gear before we had a full crew to manage the work. Now what?"

Jillian decided to stay out of the sex lives of others. "You offer the material suppliers an incentive. Add them to the invitation list for the open house. I'll make some calls to see if there are any jobbers—cloth shops—looking for work. It will be an investment, but worth it. How are your designs coming for nightgowns? Who do we have to model them?"

"Not you, that's for certain. I will not have my wife parading around in her nightie in front of buyers. I am embarrassed to ask any woman to show herself like that. We'll use sketches of anything not classified as outer-wear. This whole thing is a nightmare," Cordell stated darkly, ripping a lace scrap from one shoulder. "Your nightmare. No one can put a fashion show and market-ing plan together in less than two weeks."

"You can. I have confidence in you. Amanda has a fleet of seamstresses sewing overtime. The only problem is where we'll put everyone. The local motel only has five rooms. That's enough for everyone but my family."

"I never wanted anyone to know I was a clothing de-signer...." Cordell stopped his prowling, and began slowly flipping through his new sketches for maternity wear. "Oh? A bedroom shortage? Huh. What do you know about that?"

She sensed that the air had shifted. She hoped he didn't think she was criticizing his home. "Cordell, I love the house. I love natural wood and stone and lots of win-dows. But we only have four bedrooms and the front porch. If we put the children on the front porch, Mother and Dad in one bedroom, Tiffany and her husband in one, and Jacqueline and her husband in the other, that just leaves one bedroom.... Or we could put all the men in one place and the women in another, but my sisters and mother will want beds."

"Oh?" Cordell was very interested in a design for a long maternity nightgown. He doodled, rounded the sketch's tummy and sketched the fabric to accommo-date a pregnant mother.

"We'll have to share the bedroom," she said finally.

"Oh. That's too bad," he murmured.

Her stomach lurched. Cordell wasn't that interested in sleeping an entire night with her. Dipping into her marketing ability, she tossed in an incentive. "You can tell me about your family. We can relate."

"You're tough. I'll think about it. I found a recipe in the computer for fried noodles. Just why do you think this catalog marketing idea is going to be such a big hit?"

"Because you are talented. You would have done the catalog in good time and been just as successful. I'm just glad that I could help speed up the process." She'd pushed him too hard, and now he didn't want her.

Cordell turned to her, set aside his sketchbook and placed his hands on her shoulders. "Jillian, you scare me. Now tell me why we aren't sleeping together in our own bed every night."

Jillian blinked, the question unexpected. She wasn't skilled in combining bedroom and business talk. She hadn't yet explored all the aspects of being friends with Cordell; he was jumping ahead of her. If she let him push her past this important building block of their marriage, they might not recover. To her, the marriage bed was a coming together of hearts and minds, then bodies. While she couldn't help responding to her grab-Cordell-now instincts, anywhere and anytime, she was very determined to have the whole marriage enchilada. "Whoops! I forgot. I promised to meet Squirrels at the bus station in a few minutes. He's going to be great on our computer marketing service. A real genius with computers. I've got to go."

Cordell's frustrated groan followed her out the door.

Nanna rocked in her tent, puffed her pipe and squinted at Cordell through the smoke. "Of course I understand. I'm a woman, aren't I, boy?"

Cordell glared at her. "Well?" he demanded. "What am I doing wrong?"

Her rocking chair creaked as she rocked and smoked and finally said, "The way I see it, this is a woman who knows her own mind, doesn't like takeovers. She let you marry her because she wanted you. But you, in your caveman style, set rules she doesn't want. The both of you are hardheaded whirlwinds, neither giving an inch.... The girl is nervous. She eats strange foods at strange times and mixes burritos and egg rolls. Maybe she can't tell the difference. They're shaped the same.... 'Course, by the way she jumped you on the porch the other day, she's just as much a bushwhacker as you are. You got to start thinking about the partner business, boy. Friendship. Relating. Sharing a part of you that you've given to no other. Get romantic. Get in tune with your emotions and get supportive. Tell her your fears, the deep, dark ones that no one else knows, not even me. Ditch the hiding-in-the-emotional-cave act. Think of your wife as a ... friend. Your best friend."

"I moved my gun rack from the living room into a bedroom. She moved my favorite recliner into the pantry and covered it with a blanket. There's plants sucking space and water everywhere. We've got a couch that looks like it's orbiting the fireplace. She's taken over my studio, moving in and creating a circus. All this in less than a week. I'm exhausted. I'm making a lot of concessions here, Nanna," Cordell said defensively, longing for his goose, trout and antlers. "I've never had a close friend ... a woman, that is. They think differently."

"It's a woman thing. The marriage bed represents to the woman a point of no return. This dates back to— well, never mind." Nanna puffed on her pipe before continuing sagely, "She gives herself on this bed to the man she wants forever. The girl is old-fashioned, and has given herself before. She's been burned once, Cordell. In a way, deep in her female mind, she's testing you, checking out if she wants to really commit to you. She's wary, and you didn't help yourself none by dumping her on your bed that first night. Now, that was a real humdinger of a bad move for a new husband. You should have really played that one different. It scared her down deep. That wrong step set into motion all sorts of nervous-bride-woman emotions in her."

Cordell ran his hands wearily down his unshaven face. He realized he needed to take care with his wife. To try to understand her. But he was exhausted, and... "She's pushy," he said finally. "I don't like seeing her eyes light up when she sees a new marketing opportunity."

"Ah!" Nanna exclaimed in a eureka-I-have-found-it tone. "You're jealous."

"I have never been jealous of a woman." Cordell glared at her, burdened with all the deep emotions and uncertainty about the future and wrong steps and choices lurking ahead of him with Jillian. The tiny, telltale vein in his forehead began to throb.

Nanna looked up at him, sadness in her eyes. "Boy, at some time you'll have to convince her that you love her. You'll have to actually say the words to your wife. It's time to let the past go."

He realized that she was speaking of the walls he'd built and strengthened since childhood... of his fear of losing a loved one. Cordell raked his fingers through his hair and paced before the campfire. "This is deep," he admitted finally, and met Nanna's eyes.

She nodded sagely. "Real deep. But I'd say she's worth the struggle. She's real old-fashioned in her way, and on the other hand, she's a today woman. You've got to fit your pieces with hers and she'll do her part in return. Cordell, honey, I don't want to hurt your feelings, but in some ways you're a real throwback. Boy, you have got to get in touch with your feminine side. All the hoopla about getting the open house ready and the catalog can be to your advantage. You can study this woman you married while she's busy showing you off."

Nanna watched Cordell stride purposefully toward his house, and shook her head. Cordell Dougald was bred of mountain men, and his instincts wouldn't allow anything but a takeover. The new Mrs. Dougald had a mulish streak that hadn't surfaced yet, and Cordell was in for a fight. Meanwhile, he was losing weight and getting more ornery, and his sweet little girl-bride was eating the world's menu. Jillian rushed out to hug Cordell in the evening dusk. Nanna smiled when she saw Cordell hungrily kiss his bride and lift her high to carry her into the house.

The morning of Nanna Bear's launch into catalog and electronic marketing, Cordell stared blankly at his wife. He slapped his sketchbook down on a desk laden with photos and cloth, and a platter of hot dogs. "Jillian, I will not pose for the cover of the catalog."

Harry, who had just entered the office studio with a long printout of new accounts, stopped. Armed with his ideas for electronic marketing, Squirrels bumped into Harry's back. Ace, carrying a huge new tripod for photographic lighting, bumped into Squirrels. The three men hovered near the door, peering into the potential danger zone.

"I'm not getting pasted all over catalogs." Cordell launched at her, before running his hands through his hair and thrusting them into his back pockets. He scanned the rugged mountains, the safe mountains, and planted his boot upon a chair. "Let's use the models—women—on the sampler."

Jillian hugged him from behind, and he allowed himself to settle into her breasts. They softly dragged upward as she stood on tiptoe to kiss his earlobe and whisper, "You're just nervous, Cordell. Posing with models doesn't affect your status as a man. Everything is just fine. Marketing at the last minute has advantages, and we have time to develop the sampler into the real thing."

Cordell shook his head, trying to understand how to communicate on two levels with a woman. He felt very sensitized himself. "When you push me around and toss out orders, you seem like, er...ah...more of an equal partner than a wife."

She nuzzled his shoulder, confusing him with the two-level communication. "You think so? Really? Wives can be partners, can't they? And friends, too?"

He preferred one-level communication, the old-fashioned kind, where he told her with his body how much he cared. While he was dealing with that, and the thought that his new relatives would be infesting his territorial cave within the day, Jillian smoothed his hair back into a ponytail. His hands encircled her waist immediately, and his eyes darkened in a way that took her breath away.

She couldn't allow Cordell to waylay her in business; she asked the man hovering at the door, "What do you think, Ace? Isn't this a great artsy designer look? We could place him on a stool, surround him with Nanna Bear models of all ages, a little open shirt— His worn jeans, and the contrast between his long, lean, dangerous male look and his feminine designs will be... dynamite," she concluded triumphantly, hugging Cordell again.

He rocked in his boots, digging the heels slightly into the braided rug, rejecting the cover-model idea. "I am not the product," he muttered, embarrassed by the focus upon him. He shook his longish hair free of the ponytail.

"Details." Jillian tossed away his reluctance with a careless wave of her hand.

Cordell noted that Harry, Ace and Squirrels were stealthily backing away from the door. Cordell closed it firmly in their faces and ignored the sight of Amanda's delighted grin. Getting his wife's attention wasn't that easy; Jillian was revved up, launching herself into marketing Nanna Bear. He reached out to snag her wrist as she whizzed by him and drew her into his arms. He wanted all her attention as he made his first attempt at relating, nurturing and supporting. "Dear heart," he said firmly, "you're doing a hell of a job. I'm proud of you."

His supportive-male role had her attention. She blinked, her eyes widening behind her glasses. He took them off and tucked them in his pocket. He wanted nothing concealing the effects of his first attempt at relating. He waited for the first volley to sink in before launching another. While he was waiting, he tried the recommended light touching, the skimming of his thumb over her jawline, her cheek, and across her eyelashes. He studied the sunlight dancing across her lashes and knew that investigating his wife was the best challenge of his life. Jillian needed conversation on two levels, personal and daily small talk. At the moment, she was more committed to launching Nanna Bear than to their marriage.

Angling for another volley to keep her busy, Cordell kissed her nose and whispered, "I know I don't talk when we make love. There hasn't been much time for experimenting. But tonight..." He quickly remembered what the book had said about tantalizing. "Tonight, when we're in our own bed, I will try."

He tried a switch back to business, alternating it with the smoothing of his hands down her backside, locking on to the dual softness beneath her denim overalls. He wanted her to be aware of him tonight, very aware and ready to commit to their marriage. He had plans for a long night of lovemaking, so deep and meaningful that after the project was finished, Jillian would be thoroughly committed to him. "Harry is doing a good job in accounting."

He drew her closer, easing her under his chin before he delivered the final coup. "Like I said, Jillian, you're doing a terrific job. I've got complete confidence in the way you're marketing Nanna Bear products. If you want me for the cover, you've got me." *Give-and-take,* Cordell repeated mentally.

He nuzzled the soft frill of silky hair that had swirled to lovingly caress his chin, the flowery scents that enfolded him sweetly. "Mmm... By the way, Jillian, do you think that when we make love, you might actually...mmm...touch me?"

"I touch you." Her uncertain whisper sounded beneath his chin.

"All over, dear heart." He smiled into the wayward, silky hair, tantalizing his mouth and nose. Her blush warmed him, and so did the tiny shiver of nervousness slipping from her body to his. "Really all over. Men have buttons, too. They're just different and accessible."

Cordell closed his eyes and wallowed in his success. He'd delivered a successful one-two punch. He could practically hear her thinking. A methodical layout artist, she was circling his approach, dissecting it, and she would see how much he cared. She'd have hours to think about everything he'd said, and his good points, and she'd be primed for his takeover tonight.

"Don't be afraid, honey bear," Jillian said soothingly, shooting straight to the heart of his ploy. "My family won't collect me."

She kissed his chest, nuzzled it, and lowered her hand to lightly claim him through his jeans. He reacted instantly, hardening against the thick fabric. Jillian stood on tiptoe to kiss him. "Thank you, Cordell. You're right. I have been shy with you, but only because I didn't want to frighten you. By the way, thank you for your support. I realize that none of this can be easy for you. You are very frightened about the showing. Don't be. I'll take care of you."

When it was put like that, in her words, Cordell understood the depth of his fear. He reached out, scooped her into his arms and held her tight. He had the sinking feeling that women were far ahead of men when dealing with emotions. No wonder men for centuries had remained outside the emotional galaxies where women seemed to rule supreme. Caves were much safer.

Jillian shyly touched him again, and Cordell tossed away his game plan. "We can do this," he murmured firmly, giving himself to her light touch.

He sucked in his breath and tried not to grab her closer as she gently explored the lengthening shape of him. "You're very... unique...." she murmured after a moment.

He stood very still, certain that he had failed to measure up to a certain feminine yardstick. Technology had replaced him, at least with his ex-wife. "Define *unique.*"

Jillian was suddenly very busy, shuffling through the ad layouts. "I just hadn't realized, uh...." she stammered. He watched fascinated by her flush and trembling fingers as she added, "Large...very large. Huh. What do you know about that? I didn't realize men were so different. Ah, I mean...you know, Cordell, my experience is rather limited with male anatomy."

A measure of confidence shot into him, lifting him inches from the floor. "Everything fits," he said smoothly, drawing her fingertips up to his mouth and suckling them one at a time. "Just like you and me. Our relationship to one another is the important thing. Like...." He struggled a bit for a proper phrase. He thought of butter and bread, then remembered one of Jillian's favorite New York hungers. "Like lox and bagels. Add cream cheese and alfalfa sprouts to that."

"I think you're romantic," she whispered shyly, her eyes darkening as her lashes fluttered.

Cordell allowed himself to grin like a Cheshire cat. He might just live through the Cling-ons' visit and the launching of Nanna Bear into high-speed marketing. All he had to do was to keep the pressure up on his wife and read more when she wasn't looking. His retreats into the studio bathroom-library were paying off.

"I have fantasies." He slid in the teaser about relating his inner dreams and emotions and waited for her reaction. This was the part where she told him that she had them, too. This tantalizing bit would titillate her further, drawing them closer. Not for the world would he tell another person that he fantasized about his wife.

"What sort of fantasies?" Jillian asked cautiously. Because she was extremely nervous, she stepped from him and picked up a hot dog slathered with mustard. She licked the mustard that was about to drip with the tip of her tongue.

Cordell groaned instantly and shivered, his body very hard. "Ones to do with you and me. Intimacy. You know...pillow talk. Candles around the bathtub. You listen. I listen. Then there's the more...active fantasies."

With that, he grabbed her hot dog and threw it out the window.

8

"Oh, sure. Give me a marketing challenge and I'm off to the races," Jillian muttered while she fussed with the models. The crowd waited in the living room, munching on her special appetizer recipes and sipping drinks. "But fantasies are a different matter."

Buffy, Jacqueline and Tiffany weren't listening. Unexpectedly, her mother and sisters had leaped at the chance to model Nanna Bear fashions. From the dressing room-bedroom, they were watching their husbands cluster with Cordell, males surveying the rugged mountains. The massive windows framed their broad shoulders, and their long legs and backsides—all taut and sheathed in denim—were outlined against the late-afternoon light. "It's been years since your father and I slept in one bed," her mother whispered, her tone dripping with excitement and a dab of lust.

Jillian glanced at her, certain that she had misunderstood. But there was no mistaking the gleam in her mother's eyes. Tiffany and Jacqueline were drooling. Jacqueline licked her lips. "I'm so glad we decided to leave the children at home this time. Don't you think that Chad has the nicest backside? He hasn't gotten one ounce of flab from working behind a desk."

"Jillian, this idea of yours to actually have us share bedrooms is delightful," Tiffany purred, smoothing out the Nanna Bear creation she was to model later. "There's just something truly old-fashioned and sweet about Cordell's designs. He must be *very* romantic. Make certain we are the very first to wear this collection, will you?"

Jacqueline twirled around slowly, allowing the eyelet-lace ruffle to swish around her ankles. "This is so much fun. Mingling with the guests, wearing these sweet designs. The fashion journalists love the lace and denims. The news media is thrilled by this backwoods marketing idea.... A new company starting, the just-married angle, the cowboy designer ... Oh, look at this, a pink ribbon sewn into the bodice. How sweet."

She frowned and fingered a tag inside her bodice. "What does *Wash With Care* mean?"

Buffy's fingers were rummaging on her chin. "Oh, no. Not a zit now, not when your father is finally paying attention to me—"

Tiffany peered closer at her mother's chin. "Buffy, I believe that is a facial hair."

Buffy issued a terrorized scream, drawing the crowd's attention toward the bedroom.

Accustomed to the theatrics of the Horton family, Jillian leaned out of the door. She smiled at the crowd. "We're just excited about this premiere showing of Nanna Bear Creations."

She leaned against the door and closed her eyes, terror seeping into her. "Fantasy. What do I know about fantasies?"

A small whiff of guilt sailed by her. She hadn't flirted with Cordell, and he hadn't missed it. So much for her skills at seducing men. The first week, they had operated on a cut-to-the-chase or sensual-greed method. The second week, she'd been exhausted by work. She kicked aside her long, eyelet lace skirt and inhaled. "He wants fantasies, I'll give him fantasies. It should be just a matter of marketing...something. Whatever that is."

She had to market herself, actually package her physical endowments in some way to tantalize her groom.

Just then, Cordell turned to look at her over the head of the woman fashion journalist who was clinging to him. Jillian's heart did a Texas two-step.

"Oh, my. Isn't Chad great-looking?" Jacqueline seemed to be having problems with her breathing.

"Look at my Ralph. He's always had the greatest ass—asset."

"I think it's cute how jeans wear at stress areas. That light color is so...highlighting. I love men in worn jeans. They exude masculinity. There is just something about seeing them sweat over an outside barbecue that turns me on. I really love a man who can work up a good sweat."

"Isn't it cute how they stick together in the midst of all the photographers and news-media people? Like a herd of quail," Buffy murmured. She smoothed the denim dress with slightly billowed sleeves and calf-length skirt that she wore. "Who would ever guess that Cordell would design a romantic fantasy like this?"

Jillian plopped on the lacy broad-brimmed hat with the streaming ribbons on her head. She had a job to do, to launch Nanna Bear Creations into catalog marketing, and she would follow through. But what did she know about intimacy, relationships, pillow talk and fantasies? Panic began to claw at her, and she plopped a mini egg roll into her mouth. Then another.

Cordell had resented her invasion of his kingdom, but she had been honest about her tendency to be competitive and her love of marketing. It was better that her abilities surfaced now than after years of loving Cordell. She'd tried not to hurt his feelings. Her powerhouse drive to succeed wasn't easy to control. The bottom line was that they were two whirlwinds, wanting different things from marriage. . . .

Her heart began tearing. Now he'd know her for what she was, and she would lose him. The only communicating they'd done for a week concerned business, invoices, orders, enlarging the plant, that sort of thing. Until he took her in his arms at night and fed her and rocked her on his lap. She'd gotten used to that treatment very easily. Courtship feeding, that process whereby the mate offers food by hand-feeding his or her partner, was a lurking addiction.

The other models moving around the room did not distract Jillian from her horrifying discovery—she hadn't tried to feed Cordell that way. She hadn't tried to entice him. He was deprived of bridal attention.

She noted for the first time that Buffy had changed her hair from an extreme, sleek style to a layered cut. She studied Buffy's lace bodice. Her mother was wearing a push-up bra and a come-hither scent. Tiffany and Jacqueline had changed their hairstyles into frothier, more feminine cuts.

Nanna eased through the crowded room carrying hot rollers and barber's scissors. She caught the chins of Buffy, Tiffany and Jacqueline in turn and tilted their heads, studying her work. She artistically lifted and smoothed with a comb. "Go get 'em."

Buffy wrapped her arm around Jillian. "You did a superb job. But, honestly, the way your husband looks at us, it's as though he's afraid we're going to kidnap you and take you back to New York."

After Cordell had seen Jillian's darkest secret in action, he'd pack her bags. She hadn't been a wife to him, not the sort he wanted. She'd ignored him—fighting for her project—and she'd taken for granted that he would be waiting for her when she got home. She smoothed her dress one last time and lifted her head. One job at a time, and then she'd work on developing Cordell's fantasy.

Cordell spoke quietly with the fashion interviewer, watching his wife over the heads of the news media. She looked perfect in the lace design—sweet, wispy, delicate and bride-ish. He'd worked for hours perfecting the design; it was his gift to her. The entire romantic collection was his gift to her.

Jillian was exhausted from working from dawn until she fell asleep sitting on his lap.

His body was showing the strain. After making love frantically for one week, Jillian was dragging home every night with barely enough energy to cuddle on his lap. She barely noticed what pasta he'd cooked for her—*al dente* wasn't that easy. She'd barely noticed that he retreated to the house during the day, sketching between cooking and grocery-shopping trips. Jillian didn't seem to notice all the work he'd put into doing their laundry. He'd had to stop himself from lingering over her lingerie.

She was so cute—the way she stepped into her clean overalls every morning. She whopped on her ball cap as if going off to war. He loved listening to her rev up the all-terrain vehicle. She was out there, an expert making his dreams come true. An artist in her way, Jillian knew when to bully and when to sweet-talk. Having his kingdom invaded wasn't that bad, especially when she stopped to lean against him and slip her hand into his back pocket. He'd grown to love the way she rested her weary head upon his shoulder.

This project was really important to her; he recognized the need of a champion to succeed. He'd set his needs aside—not that easy, when she cuddled on his lap—because he didn't want to overtax her.

Sharing a bathroom with a woman was a different matter. He'd grown neurotic about the toilet seat, worrying about it when he was at the plant, wondering if he'd put it down. But all those sweet, tantalizing scents in the morning and at night made it worthwhile. A damp lace bra hitting him the face in the mornings was... welcoming, he decided. Like a little sensual caress in his formerly dark, cold cave. He hadn't been caressing her lately—she was too tired, and he wanted her to conserve her stamina for when they were totally alone.

She loved him. Could he give her what she needed to stay with him?

Dear heart, I don't know why you stay with me, his father had said after the bank turned down his loan application.

Because you're the best man I know. And because I love you. Cordell's mother had never failed to believe in sunshine and miracles and his father. Cordell had seen them sitting by the fire that night, holding hands and rocking. Then, without a word, they'd risen and gone to their bedroom, closing the door.

Every touch between his parents had meant deep affection. The following morning, his father had whistled and his mother had blushed. Cordell frowned at the woman pressing too close to him. His close space was reserved for one woman—his wife. He hoped that his marriage would become as strong as his parents'.

Jillian had been shocked by his mention of intimacy, touching and fantasies. There she was, exiting the dressing room-bedroom, dressed in the ankle-length lace dress with the ruffles around the bodice. The tendrils of her hair quivered on her neck, lit by the lamps.

She looked little like a marketing whiz, throwing darts at a target. She concentrated that way, she had explained—after a dart lodged into the target at his shoulder.

George elbowed him. "Watch the girls do their stuff. They were born to make business deals go down. Watch them circulate with the press. They'll have any critic eating out of their palms in minutes."

Cordell ignored the big-hatted woman who had looped her arm through his. He focused on his wife. Another woman with overripe perfume draped herself against him. He was too busy scouting the lay of the land, watching his wife, to notice.

Excitement layered the room. The first layer was for the launching of Nanna Bear. The other layer was not visible, yet clung heavily to his senses. His male in-laws were watching their wives with flaring nostrils and overheated bodies.

Jillian met his gaze; the other people in the room vanished. Cordell began walking toward her, unaware that he was dragging along the woman latched to him. He realized that while watching his wife he had eaten a mushroom—fungus. He smiled absently at a reporter and downed several drinks from a tray, washing away the taste. Jillian had worked so hard, and now they could begin their marriage.

They needed a few days away from everything. To relax. To relate. To find intimacy. He realized suddenly that he hadn't cared about relating and intimacy with other women, only with Jillian. He wanted to make her a part of himself and himself a part of her. He wanted this relationship to last forever.

He glanced at Buffy, who was hanging on George's arm, and at Tiffany and Jacqueline in their husbands' arms, and knew that he couldn't perform his husbandly role under the same roof as his relatives.

Cordell downed another drink as a new fear arose to smite him. After tossing Jillian on the bed their first night together, he didn't want to make another mistake—like not performing. He began to feel pressured, and knew then the depth of a bridegroom's ultimate fear.

Just then, George moved closer and murmured, "That's my little girl. See how she's showing off your sketches, marketing your company. Don't forget we want those exclusive rights if you change your mind. When she sold her Horton stock to invest in you, I knew that anything you did would sell. Jillian has turned down loads of marketing jobs. But for you and your company, she invested her inheritance and stock, and went back to doing what she should be doing. Gad, it's good to see her involved in marketing again. She always was a genius, my little girl. A real eye for stocks in the retail business. She's pretty wealthy in her own right, you know."

The taste of the mushroom-fungus rose slowly upward in Cordell's throat. His little wife had secrets of her own. He didn't relish his "wealthy" wife supporting him.

Jillian traced Cordell's path to her. She winced when he shook aside the women clinging to him. He loomed over her suddenly, his eyes narrowed and his jawline clenched. "What's this about investing your life savings in my company?" he demanded, his fingers locking onto her arm. "The money in your checking account was bad enough."

In this mood, Cordell looked perfect for the part of the pirate who had kidnapped her in her fantasy. She'd just gotten to the fantasy point where she tied him to the bed with lace. She decided then that she should have told him about what Harry had discovered. Nanna Bear Creations needed shoring up, and quickly, especially with the demands placed on it by her advertising campaign. "I am your wife. It's logical that I help when necessary. It was more personal than that... a matter of honor... I'm no less honorable than you are, Cordell. I wanted to give my husband an old-fashioned dowry."

"Dowry? Huh. I never considered a bride-price. I never gave your father one horse. Women do not support men," he said too softly. He braced his legs apart, folded his arms over his chest and scowled down at her. "It isn't right."

His bristling male image caused her to hurry. "Cordell, you have to understand. It was more of a loan to expand Nanna Bear."

"You missed that little detail," he said in a heavy, ominous tone. She looked down at the note he had slapped in her hand. "Try that little kink, dear heart," he told her challengingly before leaving her.

Meet me at the Downtown Motel. Room 5. Bring your toothbrush.

Hours later, dressed in a trench coat and nothing else, Jillian knocked on the door of room 5. The launching of Nanna Bear into advertising and catalogs was certain to be a success. Cordell's designs were so romantic that every woman's heart had melted. They were all eager to be among the first to wear the collection. Jillian had made an overseas contact, and had plans for a spring Paris show.

But first, she had to soothe Cordell's wounded pride. She shot a glance at Slough Foot's deserted streets and at the cars parked in front of the hotel. Cordell's truck couldn't be missed; the entire town would be gossiping that he was having an affair.

Jillian tingled with excitement and anticipation; having Cordell as a lover was more exciting than a good marketing plan. Nanna's battered truck was safely hidden in the stand of pines. The door opened, and Cordell's large hand reached out to drag her into the candlelit room. He was dressed in jeans, unsnapped at the waist. Droplets from his shower gleamed on his wide, hair-flecked chest, just as they did when they first met. She loved that look, as though all she had to do was to reach and—

"A little loan, huh?" he repeated ominously. She shivered, suddenly aware of how Wyoming nights could be very chilling on bare backsides.

She stared at the flowers that filled the room, and at the bed's turned-down satin sheets. "I forgot, Cordell. I apologize. It was a necessary step that needed to be taken quickly. I made that decision—"

"Without asking me, your husband."

She'd hurt him. "Cordell…" She touched his arm and found that he was staring down at her breasts, which were slightly revealed.

"Good Lord, woman. What are you doing running around naked?" he demanded.

She took a deep breath. The male mind traveled a crooked course, traveling from business to emotions to the sudden sensuality glowing in his eyes. His fingertips smoothed the lapel of the raincoat, just touching her breast, and she forgot to breathe. She resorted to fluttering her lashes in a flirtatious way.

He blinked with surprise and muttered, "I can't make love to you with your family panting away in the next room. They are a hot bunch, once you get to know them."

"They're rediscovering romance," she whispered as Cordell began to unbutton her raincoat. "What will people think about your truck in front of the motel? Should you move it?"

Cordell had unbuttoned the raincoat and was easing it away from her. His breath sucked in when he noted that she wore only a black garter belt and hose. Her red stiletto heels gleamed in the candlelight. Scented candles, she noted. Ylang-ylang—very erotic. There was fruit, and champagne cooling in an ice bucket. Flowers spilled everywhere. Her heartbeat tripped. Remembering what Cordell had said about touching him, Jillian braced herself and reached—

"I've got a real problem here, Jillian," he stated rawly after her capture and exploration of him. He stepped out of his jeans, looking all male and aroused. "Are you ready to share my bed? Like married people do?"

"This is fantasy? I thought it was games, not reality," she managed as he lifted her easily in his arms.

For a moment, Cordell looked embarrassed. "I've never wanted to go to a motel room with anyone else, dear heart. It's a new experience for me."

"It's very romantic," she whispered, clinging to him. She'd never considered herself to be seductive, yet now she desperately wanted to try her untapped skills.

"I thought about cutting out footprints and making a path to our bed. But we have visiting family. No telling who would turn up."

"You can do that some other time," she managed as he laid her down and spread himself over her.

He closed his eyes and breathed unevenly. He moved gently upon her, sliding his hands down her body, touching lightly here, pressing gently there. He smoothed down her garter belt. "I wondered if you were wearing one of these all night."

"Just for you." She smoothed his hair and kissed his eyelashes. "Cordell, the collection was very romantic. Much more romantic and feminine than your other work."

"Mmm . . ." He very carefully laid his head upon her breasts. "Wait until you see the nightgown and maternity collection."

Despite the tenderness growing between them, Jillian shocked herself by demanding, "Cordell Dougald, I must have you. I have waited so long for you. I ache for you."

He kissed the tip of her breast, suckling it. She glanced at his mouth closing over her breast and shook. For an instant, she visualized a tiny mouth, Cordell's baby, taking nourishment from her. Emotions of sensuality merged with deeper, more primitive ones, and the blend confused her. Thoughts of lying beneath Cordell flipped over, and she saw herself taking him boldly. She pushed aside her submissive past and arched her body up to his mouth.

"You need me," he murmured in a very pleased tone.

She shivered, locking him to her. "In all ways, Cordell. But . . . ah . . . right now, I can't seem to be very logical about discussion. I want to . . . ah . . . to take you wildly . . . ah . . . in not the conventional position, if you know what I mean. Are you frightened?"

"Hell, no," he exclaimed, with a tone she hoped was delighted. Then he added, "I'm yours, fantasy woman."

Fantasy woman. He knew how to compliment and encourage his wife. Jillian decided to try her flirtatious routine later; he seemed so fascinated when she licked her lips and fluttered her eyelashes. She decided then and there that Cordell needed her to flirt with him. But much later on their agenda.

She eased him onto his back and straddled him. "You're wearing your heels, dear heart," he reminded her gently. But it was too late; he was hers, filling her, loving her.

There she was, a primitive woman bearing down on her lover and taking him. She was strong, hot and well loved, sought by Cordell's hunger, which matched her own. Jillian released every primitive emotion she had, let go of her inhibitions and took Cordell quickly. He was hers for the claiming, hers to drag back to her cave and to savor....

Quivering in the aftermath of her desire, she rested limply upon him, surprised when Cordell gently turned her beneath him and kissed her in that soft, coaxing, romantic way of his. "You're cute, hot stuff," he whispered in her ear, surging into her and moving for the perfect fit.

Cuddled up to Cordell later, Jillian listened to his slowing heartbeat and stroked the hair on his chest. The candles flickered in the room. Cordell had covered the two of them with a sheet. His breathing had changed, and he was sleeping. He held her tightly in his arms, as though fearing she would leave. Jillian snuggled down closer, locked in her thoughts.

There she was, pushing and shoving Cordell in her powerhouse-woman way. She'd jumped him in his fantasy, and she hadn't exactly been gentle. She'd been shocking in her hunger.

He smoothed her back, ran his fingertips across her nipple and whispered sleepily, "Don't think so hard. We'll be just fine. We just need time."

"You think so, Cordell?" she asked, pleased that he was aware of her doubts and wanted to soothe her.

"Sure."

"Thank you for supporting me this week. For cooking and cleaning and letting me push you around."

"Sure." He stretched and yawned sleepily, then reclaimed her against him. He fit his fingers into hers, just the way she liked, his thumb smoothing the back of her hand. His pinkie settled very firmly between her ring and littlest finger.

He seemed so mellow, she decided the opportunity was ripe to try her first effort at pillow talk. "Cordell, exactly how did you feel about Portia and Alicia?"

"They were okay. More friends than..." His fingertips stroked her flushed cheek and her throat. He circled her ear. "You've got the cutest ears. Tasty, too. When you get mad, they turn pink."

She realized fully how much she had yelled at him this past week. "Cordell, I am so sorry that I yelled at you... but you can be so—"

"Dictator-like?" he supplied. "Your father gifted me with that information from you."

"You're not that bad. You just have this awful clammish streak. You retreat into your emotional cave and bristle like a bear when I come near you. I've been trying to realize that you need time alone to cope with events—like me."

He snorted. "Men don't go around spouting off about their emotions."

"You seem to do rather well when you don't like something about business."

"Business is business. You push. It's okay," he murmured, nuzzling her ear as his hand smoothed the curves of her body.

"So you don't mind me entering your kingdom-cave...er, your business? Ah...you really don't mind me investing in Nanna Bear, do you?"

"Well..." He nudged his heavier thigh between hers. "Can we talk about this later?"

Here she was, in his fantasy cave—one he had carefully decorated—dealing with realities. Jillian felt guilty and aroused as Cordell began kissing her. "I'm going to try to talk more when we make love," he whispered against her breasts. "But I just may get carried away and forget. Don't expect too much communication when we're like this—I mean, talk. It's all in my mind, though, even if I don't say it."

Fascinated with the direction of his mind, and alternating that with the arousing distraction of his mouth and hands, Jillian asked, with all the verbiage she could summon up, "Mmm?"

He kissed the tip of her breast, suckled it into a peak and nibbled it very lightly. "Oh, things like...how pink and cuddly you are now, when just a minute ago you were very hot."

She decided courtesy demanded that she return his compliment. "You're sweet."

He snorted against her belly button. "No one has ever said that before. Some people say I terrorize them. Sometimes I do it just because they're expecting me to."

"Ah...just where are you going, honey bear?" she asked breathlessly, her body rippling with anticipation of where he would put his lips next.

"No telling. I'm working on this intimacy thing, and I am very committed to succeeding. Let's just keep talk ing. Though I seem to be losing my train of thought. You've got skin that smells like flowers, cute little nipples that stand up... You wear a heavier bra and a heavy shirt when you go jogging. A jacket, too," he ordered firmly as Jillian began to squirm, her passions reaching the boiling point.

For just a heartbeat, a shadow slid by Jillian. Cordell had secrets; he was hoarding his darkness. She sensed that he feared losing her. She ached for the small boy who had lost his family, for the man who had not known love and did not trust it. They would have time. Then she gave herself to the passion ruling them....

In the hour preceding dawn, Cordell rested his head upon Jillian's breasts and cuddled her closer. "Dear heart, you do a good job."

She stroked his hair and kissed his temple. "I didn't know two people could fit in a bathtub."

He nuzzled her softness and smiled lazily. "I like your go-for-it attitude."

"Oh, dear. I am rather shocking, aren't I?"

"I like it." His fingers drifted through her hair, smoothing it. "Now tell me about your ex-husband. He got a big thrill out of making you feel inadequate, didn't he? He probably liked a submissive partner."

A host of bad memories sailed by her. Jillian held Cordell very tightly. He was her new life. "He couldn't stand my competitive side. I guess I made him feel inadequate. That was why it was so important for me to be truthful with you. I just can't seem to stop going for business challenges, rather like a hungry trout."

"You know how I felt when you took me on the porch that day?" Cordell whispered in her ear. "Like you needed me to come home to. People have needed me for support or money, but no one has needed me for me. I like that.''

She was so happy with him that she turned quickly, reaching for him. Cordell let out a pained yell and gripped her knee, easing it away from his injured body. ''Watch that.''

''I apologize. Men are so delicate.'' She stroked his chest to soothe him. ''I'll try to be more careful with you.''

''But you're going to sleep with me, right?'' He wrapped his arms and legs around her tightly. ''We'll work on the elbows-and-knees thing as we go along. Practicing will help.''

An hour later, she awoke dreamily to hear Cordell murmur, ''Dear heart...'' He pulled her body to him in a gentle claiming. ''I've missed you.''

She pressed close to Cordell. ''I love you.''

He was silent too long. The small hope that he would reply in kind began to sink. She held him tightly, keeping him from his shadows. ''Make love to me, Cordell.''

''Pushy woman.'' His smile moved against the curve of her neck.

''I'm in for the long haul, buddy,'' she returned, stroking the taut nape of his neck. She eased her fingers through his hair and looked into his shadowy eyes. She ached for him, loved him. ''I'm not going anywhere.''

Cordell braced himself over her, studying her in the shadows of dawn. His thumb traced her cheekbone ''You're a stubborn cuss, once you lock on to an idea You think you've got what runs between us figured out?''

''I know it's good,'' she whispered.

''Very good.'' His lips lowered to smooth hers; th moment was tender. ''Don't leave me....''

The words tore her heart, wounding her with their uneven timbre. Whatever his pain, he preferred to meet it alone. "Come here," she whispered, rising to enfold him. "You're mine. I do so love you."

9

Late July hovered, cool and sweet, on the mountain morning. Preparing for their evening meal before he began sketching his country-brides collection, Cordell watched the fingers of pasta extrude from the machine. He thought about adding a new line with fringe to Nanna Bear's growing collection. He liked working at home, though having his wife work at the factory sat uneasily upon him. She was already there, laying out a fall-and-winter catalog.

The catalog business was successfully launched, and Jillian and he had had time to camp, to explore his ranch and each other. His marriage should be comfortable; it wasn't. Every day he noticed a disquiet in his bride. Jillian was sending signals; all he had to do was interpret them.

Cordell lifted the heavy coil of linguine strands from the platter to hang it from a drying peg. Now, having adjusted to the intricacies of married life and relating, he barely missed his fish, his goose and his antlers.

Cordell cleaned the kitchen briefly, checked to see if he had enough fresh tomatoes to start the spaghetti sauce in the afternoon, and pumped hand cream into his palms. He had learned after repairing fence lines and chopping winter wood that a married man needed to take good car of his hands. There was hand-holding involved, as well as treasuring his bride's responsive body.

An uneasy quiet encircled him as a breeze trembled in the leaves of the aspens beyond the window. *He was losing her.*

Cordell glanced around their home, filled now with things they had collected together. His old recliner looked comfortable in a shadowy corner, a basket full of his sketchbooks beside it. A faint feminine scent enclosed him, and he frowned. *Something was wrong between them.*

He wandered into the well-lit office area and sat down at his sketching table. He ran his pencil across the paper, listening to the sound and waiting for the ideas to fall before him. *Jillian was waiting for something, and he wasn't supplying it.*

Cordell moved to the computer and turned it on. An immediate notice of electronic mail popped onto the screen. "E-mail" from Jillian usually involved asking his opinion about a current marketing plan or what he planned for a fabric. She used e-mail so as not to disturb his creative time; he could check it at will. The message read *I'm taking time off. Leaving at noon.*

He nodded, still trying to find the reason he was uneasy with Jillian now. When they made love, or in the tender moments when she snuggled next to him, he sensed that she was waiting. Waiting for what? He tapped into the computer file to check on Harry's accounting files. Cordell liked the pie graphs showing how much profit had increased due to the catalog and electronic marketing. He tapped into Squirrels' computer ordering service and noted the steady orders jumping onto the screen. Silver conchos added to the fringe idea on denim would be—

Cordell held his breath and checked his e-mail from Jillian again. "Taking time off?"

There it was—an e-mailed Dear John letter from his bride.

Things had been too good for him.

"We'll see about that, dear heart," he murmured, jamming on his western hat and his leather gloves.

The other Dear John letters hadn't made him saddle Nightmare with grim determination. He hadn't fought for another woman; this wife he was keeping. Cordell pushed away the anger and found his fears lying in wait for him, and his heart beginning to tear.

He passed a bouquet of roses on his way to the door and grabbed one for good luck. Flowers. Jillian loved them, and lace. He'd wanted to design a new lace just for her. Funny thing, how a flower could boost a man's shaken life...

He saddled Nightmare slowly, forcing himself not to run to the truck and race to her. He tempered his fear by moving automatically and riding slowly toward the plant. While he rode, he went over potential problem areas in his mind. Jillian seemed to miss her family at times. He could move to New York to make her happy... or the Cling-ons could invade his territory again.

Why had he awakened during the night to find her looking at him so sadly?

What did her worried, curious glances mean?

Deep in thought, preparing what she was going to say to Cordell, Jillian walked toward her all-terrain vehicle. All the ingredients of a good marriage weren't in hers. She inhaled the fresh mountain air, scented by pine and fir trees. Deer looked at her as they crossed a meadow and a playful shout went up in the day-care center.

She ached to have him say, "I love you." She knew that he was trying for her. But if she had to ask him to say the words, they would be tarnished. She wanted Cordell to say them and mean them.

He showed her with his body, savoring her while they made love, with the playful boyish streak she was certain no one else had seen. Yet ...

Through better marketing, Cordell's romantic designs would be in Paris soon; his growing bridal collection would take Europe by storm. She'd done her job, loving the excitement and the challenge.

She loved Cordell madly, without conditions.

Her emotion had not been returned in full. He did not trust her enough to share his shadows.

In the quiet of the night, with his arms holding her and his breath teasing her cheek as he slept, she ached for him. She needed time to refresh, to think about how to face this aspect of their life. Amanda had noticed Jillian's uneasiness and had offered a solution that worked for her....

Nightmare walked out of the pines. Cordell's forearms were crossed on the saddle horn, the reins loose in his gloved hands. The western picture, complete with the glowering cowboy-husband, his hat low on his head, sent a trickle of fear up the nape of her neck. He looked down at her, his eyes piercing the shadows made by his hat. She noted that beneath his morning stubble, the hard, grim line of his mouth had returned. She mourned for the crooked, boyish grin pasted on the husband she'd left sprawled in bed this morning. The only softening touch was the rose tucked in his shirt pocket.

"Oh, hi," she managed, trying a wobbly smile up at him.

"Morning."

"Okay, okay," she said quickly. Cordell would not begin a topic in which he felt he was due an apology. "I'm going on a retreat."

"That's real nice," he said easily. The grim lines bracketing his mouth deepened.

She backed away from Nightmare as Cordell guided him closer. "I just decided this morning."

Cordell stuck out his boot in the stirrup. "Hop on."

When she hesitated, Cordell simply reached and plucked her from the ground. He installed her across his lap. She realized how he had tempered his strength when handling her.

While he guided Nightmare to a small, rippling stream near the house, Jillian planned her explanation. She hadn't realized that he could guide a horse and cradle her firmly against him. She decided to start with a tiny kiss to his throat.

"Don't start anything you can't finish," he warned, swinging down to the earth. He lifted her in his arms and carried her to a fallen log. He sat down, still holding her. "What's this about a retreat?"

"I don't want to hurt you, Cordell. But there are things that I must sort out alone."

"Such as?"

"You don't have to be so grim. Women need free time to think, just like men do."

"I thought you did that when you exfoliated."

This was going to be more difficult than she thought. She stroked his jaw; the stubble-covered surface was unrelenting, contracting beneath her palm. Cordell was either bristling or hurting. He hoarded his emotions, which was one of her problems. She had to deal with how she felt. Honesty with herself was something she had learned long ago. "I want to think about us. Where we're going.

I need to think about us without you. I ordered paints and canvas boards to occupy my hands while I'm thinking. Amanda thought it was a good idea, and I've always wanted to paint. I could paint you a goose, or a fish while I'm camping."

"I see."

"Big guy, you're not helping here."

"What's wrong with us?" He sincerely wanted to know, and she didn't want to hurt him; she wanted to think about how to arrange her wording, about how—

"I want more for us. I just haven't worked out the details yet. You make thinking very hard when I'm at home with you... or making love in the barn... or on a picnic blanket... or when I'm thrilled with something new you've done.... It's just darn hard to think around you, Cordell. Then, when I'm at work, even darts won't cut it. Amanda says she sometimes goes off for a holiday by herself, and her husband understands."

"He does, does he?" Cordell's tone did not show any fraction of understanding. He sounded as if he planned to run down Amanda's husband and call him out.

"Yes. Ah... do you realize that you are holding me very tightly?"

"I don't want you to get away," he answered roughly, easing his embrace, and she knew it was true.

"It's called trust, Cordell. You'll have to trust me."

Her hand began to sweat around the emergency flare. Camping without Cordell was frightening. He'd packed her gear, demonstrated how to use the flare and ordered her not to wait if she saw a bear. Or a coyote. Or a cougar.

He'd been determined to frighten her, and she'd been just as determined to carry through with her time away from him.

Jillian scanned the mountain's evening shadows and sat upright in her sleeping bag when a huge image appeared out of the pines. A bear foraging for food... Cordell had taught her about the emergency flare. She fired it too soon. The fiery rocket shot across the meadow and into the stand of pines near the shadow. The shadow dropped to the ground with a yell and a curse.

A frightened night bird knocked over her new painting.

"Cordell?" she asked, her heart leaping wildly with fear. Wounded bears were legendary for their bad tempers; Cordell could be worse. She realized she hadn't seen him in a truly bad temper since they'd been married. He'd been irritated, grouchy and nettled, and he yelled sometimes. But Cordell had never really erupted.

She'd never seen that side of him. But with the rocket glare sweeping just past his startled face, he could be a tad angry.

He stood slowly, dusting off his body with his hat and stalking toward her. "In the sky, dear heart," he muttered. "The idea is to signal me if you need me. Do you?"

"Always," she returned instantly. Then she added, "But not tonight. I'm on a retreat. What are you doing here? It's only been a few hours."

"That's all I can take," he muttered, sinking down beside her and enfolding her with his arm. He rocked her gently and handed her a rose. "I miss you. But," he added firmly, "I trust you."

"You're afraid I'll leave you."

Cordell lifted her onto his lap, sleeping bag and all. "I'd come after you. You're mine," he whispered unevenly against her temple.

"Yes, I've always been, from the moment we met. You're my other half, my life, Cordell. But you won't share the shadows with me. At times you close me out and it hurts."

He gathered her closer, staring at the fire. "I never want to hurt you, dear heart. There are just some things that are too dark to share with you. Since we've been married, they're coming back."

"I am here for you, Cordell Dougald," she whispered, nuzzling the familiar scent of his throat. "You are mine now, and nothing can take you away."

"I didn't want to love you."

Her heart began tearing, pain ripping through her.

"But I do. There's the joy of it, and then the pain."

Her heart, formerly in pieces, lightened. "You know I love you. With love between us, anything is possible."

"You are my sunshine," he said slowly. "The sweet honey-berry of my heart. Each day with you begins new and fresh and filled with surprises. I'm proud of you, too. Though you can push a little hard sometimes. I really didn't like that rocket shooting at me. I had visions of being skewered to a tree."

"I am sorry, Cordell. But you did tell me to shoot it when I was alarmed." She remembered the spats that came from working together, and the tender making-up. He still mourned his stuffed goose. His traumatic loss of it, the fish and the antlers arose periodically. Lately she'd been suspecting he was teasing her, ambushing her to start a tiff, so that then he could grab and kiss her.

"Shoot it into the sky. Not at anything that moves. Did you miss me?" he demanded, and she sensed he needed reassurance.

"Terribly."

"Come home, and let's lie in front of the fire. Or let me in that sleeping bag with you. I need to hold you without a wad of down between us."

When they were lying, watching the campfire die, her back spooned against Cordell's chest, he said, "It's coming back to me. How much my parents loved each other. A look from you, or a word. A feeling deep within me. It all makes me remember. I've stashed away those memories, because they hurt. Now here they are, and I don't know how to handle them. It's like the hurt waited all these years that I've been working hard to build the business. Waited to come out. I wish they could have met you, dear heart."

She held very still. All the love she wanted, she heard in his words now as he continued, "Times were too hard. My father was a struggling rancher. Work took its toll on my mother. I promised myself that I'd never let my wife do without, or work. Then you come along. The career woman. The marketing whiz, with enough talent to knock me flat."

She noted the humor in his tone and treasured his soft, sweet kiss. "One can only market a very good product with this amount of success," she returned modestly.

"My romantic designs since we married have been because of you."

"Truly?" she asked, realizing the depth of his emotions. She remembered the delicacy of his new sketches, compared with the boldness of the old.

"Truly. I knew I had to make you mine from the moment I saw you standing in the hallway and carrying that size-seven shoe box. I was so impatient to get you into my bed and so busy coping with you ruining my cave that I didn't realize love had come to me. But it had, well and good, dear heart. Could we make love now?'' Cordell asked with tender impatience as he rolled her to her back.

"When?'' she whispered against his kiss as he settled upon her, burgeoning against her waiting softness. He kissed her palm as she smoothed his cheek.

"I suspected it right along, because I never cared enough to put up with anyone's antics like yours. Living with a female powerhouse isn't easy. But glimpses of my mother and father came back to me, the love shining between them, and I knew it was like that with me.''

She traced the outline of his beloved rugged face, smoothing his rumpled hair, and asked the question that she had been longing to since meeting him. She wanted to know everything about him, and yet knew he would keep his darkest secrets. She would tend him and love him and keep him in peace as they made their way through life. "Cordell, when and why did you decide to become a designer?''

His husky voice was smothered against her throat, and his finger and thumb were finding the sensitive tip of her breast. Passion was riding him now, the need to have her hold him close and warm in the tightest way. Against the starlit sky, Cordell's bare shoulders were broad and safe and hers. She latched her fingertips to him, her body humming to be joined with his . . .

Cordell filled her suddenly, unable to wait. Then he lay very still, as if he had captured what he wanted most. "I love you,'' he whispered against her lips.

A tear came slipping down his cheek to dampen her lips. Jillian knew that they were home. . . .

Epilogue

━━◆━◆━━

Five years later, Cordell stood in the midst of a Parisian fashion show. He was surrounded by reporters, fashionmongers, flashing cameras—and George Horton. His father-in-law proudly wanted the world to know that he had first option on Nanna Bear's exclusive rights.

Shaken by the hustle and demands of his first show, Cordell had tossed away civility. He kept his Stetson firmly in place. There he was, looming over the press, with a daughter dressed in Nanna Bear Junior Fashions sitting on the crook of each arm. Lelani, at three years old, had raven curls, while four-year-old Emily—named after both his mother and Jillian's—was very fair. Each girl wrapped one arm around their father's neck and hugged Nanna Bear dolls, whose dresses matched their own. Cordell was a whiz with dainty pinafores and matching bloomers with lace.

Lelani was already showing signs of inheriting Cordell's impatience. She leveled a glare at a model who touched her daddy. "Let go. He's mine," Lelani ordered fiercely.

"Yeah. He's ours and Mommy's," Emily chimed in, just as fiercely.

Jillian hurried through the crowd to her family. She was accustomed to smoothing over public scenes. Paris was not ready for Cordell, or their daughters. "What are you doing?" he had demanded of a model who slithered next to him. "I don't need any, lady. *I am a married man*," he had said in an old-fashioned outraged tone. Silence had stretched over the successful debut of Nanna Bear Creations in Paris.

When Jillian reached his side, Cordell scowled down at her. His indignant expression matched his daughter's fierce frowns. "She out-and-out touched me, Jillian."

Jillian smiled at a passing reporter. "Cordell, could we talk about this later?"

With a delicacy inherited from her mother, Emily moved into the silence. "Daddy said he loves his girls and he started sewing dresses when he was just a little boy for his sister. His mom and dad worked long hours and they were tired. He cooked and cleaned, and sewed dresses for his sister. Her name was Sissy. He loved her, and he loves us. Isn't that right, Daddy?" she asked, touching Cordell's cheek, which was turning a nice shade of pink.

"Okay. Okay. I sewed doll dresses when I was five or six," he muttered. "It's not that easy to relate to girls, you know. I'm trying new techniques—a modern sort of a father, you know. But don't think that I'm tossing away my fishing and camping trips. We need our family retreats," he stated firmly. "Together."

True to the new give-and-take style he had adopted, Cordell added, "I liked that last goose you painted. It was, ah . . . modernistic."

The press surged to enfold the Dougalds, and Cordell gathered his daughters protectively closer, glaring at the crowd. "Do your stuff, dear heart. Because in about two minutes I am leaving this circus, business or not."

"Yeah," Emily and Lelani chimed in together. Then Lelani continued. "While you were busy with the models and talking business, Daddy said if we were good, he'd make us special doll dresses. You only get a black see-through nightie. But if you're good, maybe he'll make something else for you. He ordered flowers sent to our room. They're not as pretty as ours at home, but he said you were a sucker for roses."

Jillian was looking at her family. Cordell, all fierce and warriorish, stood with his lace-bedecked daughters in his arms. Emotion welled up in her, and tears brimmed in her eyes.

"Well . . . uh . . ." he muttered, obviously caught in the act of planning out his latest seduction of her. He was getting truly creative, and there were moments when he stunned her by telling her what was in his thoughts—a memory of his father kissing his mother, of her nursing Sissy and the love filling their poor home. He bent to receive Jillian's kiss. "Is everything okay? I mean with you? Is this what you wanted?" he asked—then shot a glare at a reporter. "Man, I am talking with my wife. She comes first, so lay off, okay?"

His expression when he looked down at her again switched to tenderness. "I love you, dear heart."

"Go get 'em, Pops," she whispered, loving him—her tall, talented Wyoming cowboy, with instincts to capture and to make loving nests for his family. The past came gently now, deepening love as he told her more of what he had shut away. She wanted his family to be in theirs, love carried on for another generation. "And then I'm grabbing you for my own and taking you back to my cave. You are mine, Mr. Dougald.''

''I like the sound of that, dear heart,'' he returned. His kiss lit up all the photographers' flashes.

* * * * *

As seen on TV!
Free Gift Offer

With a Free Gift proof-of-purchase from any Silhouette® book, you can receive a beautiful cubic zirconia pendant.

This gorgeous marquise-shaped stone is a genuine cubic zirconia—accented by an 18" gold tone necklace.

(Approximate retail value $19.95)

Send for yours today...
compliments of *Silhouette®*

MILLION DOLLAR SWEEPSTAKES
AND EXTRA BONUS PRIZE DRAWING

SWP-ME96

SILHOUETTE®

Desire®

CELEBRATION 1000

is on its way
in April, May and June 1996!

Join us for the celebration of Desire's 1000th book!
We'll have

- Book #1000, *Man of Ice* by Diana Palmer in May!
- Best-loved miniseries such as **Hawk's Way** by Joan Johnston, and **Daughters of Texas** by Annette Broadrick
- Fabulous new writers in our Debut author program, where you can collect **double** Pages and Privileges Proofs of Purchase

Plus you can enter our exciting Sweepstakes for a chance to win a beautiful piece of original Silhouette Desire cover art or one of many autographed Silhouette Desire books!

SILHOUETTE DESIRE'S CELEBRATION 1000
...because the best is yet to come!

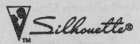